Blatherskite

Blatherskite

MARIAN POTTER

William Morrow and Company
New York   1980

Library of Congress Cataloging in Publication Data

Potter, Marian.
  Blatherskite.
  Summary: A talkative 10-year-old, living in rural Missouri in the 1930's, becomes the heroine of her family and community by putting her wagging tongue to good use.
  [1. Country life—Fiction.   2. Missouri—Fiction]
I. Title.
PZ7.P853Bl   [Fic]   80-18450
ISBN 0-688-22249-8
ISBN 0-688-32249-2 (lib. bdg.)

1

Maureen had great confidence in the United States mail, although she had never received anything unexpected at the postal window. After school she ran ahead of her brothers toward the store. The sign above the wide porch read, *General Merchandise, S. P. Stackhouse, prop.* In smaller letters below were the words, *U. S. Post Office, Dotzero, Missouri.* Maureen was proud of Dotzero's post office, which was as good as any in a big town or even a city. Lots of places back in the hills, off the railroad, didn't have post offices.

"Wait for me," she called to Mit and Walter. "I'm going to ask for mail."

"Won't be any. We've got to get over our bridge. The creek will be up from the rain," Mit said. He was the oldest and thought he knew everything.

"There might be something . . . no telling what." As Maureen opened the door, Walter started to follow her. He was seven, three whole years younger than she, and tagged after her a lot. Maureen knew that if he came into the store, he'd get fidgety and not let her talk to Mrs. Stackhouse. "Stay out here on the porch, Walter. I'll only be a minute."

Maureen wasn't sure of the meaning of *prop.* on the store sign. If Mr. Sterling Price Stackhouse was the prop of general merchandise, then Mrs. Stackhouse must be the prop of her husband. She was his store clerk *and* the Dotzero postmistress, both at the same time.

Mrs. Stackhouse wasn't much taller than Maureen, but she was a lot wider. Her head showed just above a pile of overalls on the dry-goods side of the store. When she saw Maureen, she hurried to the postal window and stepped up on a stool to reach a mail pigeonhole.

"Any mail for McCracken?" Maureen asked the routine question.

Mrs. Stackhouse puffed for breath as she looked carefully at an envelope. "Well, yes. It's from St. Louis, came in on Number 3 this morning. It could be from your Uncle Millard." She tapped the letter in the palm of her hand as she came out from behind the postal window.

Studying Maureen's thin cotton dress and worn slippers, she said, "Tell your mother we have two new bolts of gingham and some heavy Buster Brown laced shoes."

"Oh, I will." Maureen tugged at her garters to pull up her cotton stockings. "She'll be in to pick out dress

6

goods. Right now I'm wearing out these patent-leather slippers and this summer dress before I outgrow 'em."

"We've got in some new barrettes, too, a whole card of nice ones."

Maureen brushed back her short black hair. "I'll have to get one. I lost mine at morning recess playing Prison Base."

"How did Dotzero School go today?" Mrs. Stackhouse asked. "I didn't see hide nor hair of a Sansoucie going up that school hill."

"They came the first day; then they quit. I sure miss walking to school with Rose Sansoucie," Maureen said. "Sansoucies and us are the only ones living across Lost Creek. Rose said they have to save their shoes for colder weather, said the little kids might come barefoot, but she wouldn't."

"Sansoucies are laying low," Mrs. Stackhouse said, with a knowing nod. "How's Alma Huckstep doing with her teaching?"

"All right, far as I know. But when it rained so hard today, there wasn't much school. There was so much thunder over the schoolhouse we felt as if we were under a washtub. It was dark, too. So I just talked out loud."

"Talked out loud! Can't she keep order?"

Mit stuck his head in the door. "Maureen! Come on! We've got to get over the creek."

Maureen held out her hand for the letter, which Mrs.

7

Stackhouse gave her as if she hated to release it. "How are your kinfolks getting along in St. Louis?"

"Tol'able, just tol'able." Maureen used her grandmother's expression. She wasn't sure what it meant, but she wanted to try it out. "We haven't heard from them for a long time. I don't remember for sure when. Easter maybe. They didn't come to Dotzero all summer. Of course, my cousins have to go to school just about all the time up there. I sure am glad—"

"Let us know how they are," Mrs. Stackhouse interrupted. "Lots of city folks are having it harder than peach pits."

Out on the porch Maureen studied the envelope. It was Uncle Millard's handwriting. The postmark read St. Louis, Missouri, September 21, 1936. Mit snatched the letter from her and put it in the pocket of his denim jacket. "I'm in charge of anything first class."

He set a fast pace down the narrow, muddy road beside the railroad track. It wasn't easy to keep up with him, especially for Maureen who talked steadily the mile and a half to Lost Creek. "Declarative, imperative, exclamatory, interrogative," she recited. Then she explained to Walter, "Those are sentences, and if you don't say things that way, then you just haven't said anything. I learned that today listening to Mit's language class."

When she had told all she knew about the types of sentences, she continued to chant the words: *declara-*

8

tive, imperative, exclamatory, interrogative. Interrogative was good for five running hops.

At the creek, a plank footbridge lurched in the churning water, blood red from the wash of hillside clay. "We can't get home over our bridge." Mit yelled to be heard over the roar of the water. "We'll have to cross on the railroad trestle. You hung around the post office too long, blabbing to Mrs. Stackhouse. You'd be there yet if I hadn't shagged you out." He turned onto a path that led through dry weed stalks up a steep railroad embankment.

Maureen watched him. Mit wouldn't coax. He'd scramble up that bank and expect Maureen and Walter to follow.

They looked up. It was an awful distance from the red water up, up to the trestle. Dotzero School, even McCrackens' house could fit under that bridge with room to spare. It had no sides. Worse yet, it had no bottom except steel supports and crossties. Maureen's head felt light when she looked up and saw the ragged gray clouds and dark sky between the ties. If the Sansoucie kids had been along, she would have been braver, just to give them courage.

There was no other way. She and Walter would have to climb up and walk across those ties. Looking up didn't make Maureen nearly as sick as looking down from the bridge through the open spaces high over the swirling water. That's when Walter got dizzy and sometimes couldn't take another step. He would walk slower and slower, then stop, like a rundown toy, right in the middle of the trestle. Maureen would have to urge him on and talk him across.

She started up the bank, but Walter lagged and looked back. Across the swift water, the opposite bank was only a few feet away. He shivered in his damp jacket. "Wait, wait a minute," he pleaded.

"Come on. Step on it, Walter," Mit ordered, "and don't look at me with those hound-dog eyes."

Walter caught up with Maureen and grabbed her sweater, trying to hold her back. "Dad will come with the mules and take us across."

"Dad's got work today, remember? He has maybe three days with the railroad extra gang that's laying side track."

Maureen shifted her heavy school books from one arm to the other. As she was three grades ahead of Walter and had more books, she liked to bring lots home. Now she wished she had left them at school. It was hard enough to take care of herself on the bridge without the burden of books. "Milton, carry my books." She used his name, which sometimes pleased him; her voice was pleading and pitiful.

"You brought 'em; you carry 'em." Mit wasn't going to give in on anything.

Maureen looked up at the tall signal beside the track.

The trestle was on the main line of the Missouri Pacific Railroad, and they never knew what might be coming. If the red-and-white signal arm at the top was straight up, no train was within a five-mile block of track. If a train *was* coming, the signal arm fell to the side to show a red light. The arm was straight up.

"There's nothing in the block, nothing coming," Mit announced.

Maureen turned to look at Walter. "No use to expect anybody to help us, Walter. You're seven, going on eight. You're not supposed to be afraid to cross the trestle after first grade. The railroad company has built this high bridge, so we might as well use it." Maureen was afraid to cross the trestle too, but she knew that once across the relief would be worth the fright.

At the bottom of the cindery embankment, Maureen stooped to pick a cluster of purple berries from a tall weed. Mit kicked down a shower of track ballast. "Keep moving," he shouted.

"I'm getting some pokeberries to make Walter some pokeberry ink. It will be good enough ink for him to learn to write with. He ought to get so he—"

"Shut up, Maureen, and come on." Mit stepped onto the bridge.

Pokeberries could be messy. Maureen tossed them aside and climbed the embankment. Carefully she fitted her speller, reader, arithmetic and language books on top of her big geography book and clasped the load to her chest for better balance. With a choppy stride, stepping on each tie, she started across.

Walter followed, brave as long as he could look down between the ties and see the tops of willow trees on the bank below. A few more steps put him over surging water. He stopped.

"Put one foot down and then the other." Mit demonstrated stepping high. "First thing you know, you're over the trestle. Don't look down at the water. Look at Maureen's heels. Step when she does."

"I have to look down," Walter wailed.

"If you don't, you might fall right smack-dab between the ties," Maureen warned.

"Hush up, Reen Peen," Mit ordered.

"Don't call me that," she muttered through tense lips.

"Don't scare Walter then," he retorted. "You can't fall between the ties, Walter," Mit called to him. "If I took a sledgehammer and tried to drive you through the space between the ties, I couldn't do it."

Walter knew it was true. But it was also true that he was fearful. He had to force his short legs over the few inches of open space between the firm timbers that supported the track.

Mit was across. He tested his pitching arm throwing bits of gravel ballast from beside the track. Walter was sure taking his time, so Mit shouted to him, "If you look down now, you'll see the sandbar this side of the bank. Don't take the rest of the day."

Two more steps and Maureen would be on solid ground. "There might be an extra freight or a signal-man's speeder coming, and it would knock us to smithereens," Maureen shrieked.

Mit pinged gravel at her feet. "Stop scaring him, Reen Peen."

"Well, once there was a fellow—tramp maybe—and he forgot to look at the block signal to see if anything was coming, and he got out on the middle of the bridge, and sure enough here came the Sunshine Special. He had to jump off into Lost Creek, only he didn't make it."

Walter's steps quickened. Firm ballast filled the awful space between the ties, and he took a deep breath. "I walked the trestle," Walter said, beaming. His smile was so broad that his eyes became sparkling slits.

"You did fine, Walter," Mit assured him.

"I walked it when I was little like him, huh, Mit?" Maureen asked.

"I don't remember. If you did, nobody was scaring the daylights out of you. You probably blabbed, blabbed all the way across."

Mit had sure turned mean since he was thirteen and in the eighth grade. He ran ahead up the lane beside the bottom field where McCracken corn had been cut and gathered into shocks. A path that was a shortcut led from the lane up the hill.

The path was red as it crossed the bank of wet, slippery clay. Then it turned grayish as it threaded its way through limestone rock ledges. Maureen and Walter took care to walk on each natural rock step, for Maureen had assured Walter that those steps brought good luck. A person was likely to have good luck anyhow, but sometimes it had to be helped along.

Mit paid no attention to the steps. Someday he might be sorry. He just wouldn't listen.

Mit was first to reach the little frame house, which showed a few traces of white paint on its gray, rain-soaked clapboards. Tisket, their fox terrier, raced from the yard to greet him. She acted as if he'd been gone a couple of years.

Maureen put her books on the back porch and went to the tire swing that hung from a branch of the oak tree in the front yard. There was a puddle of water in the worn spot under the swing. But it didn't matter. Maureen's slippers were already wet as sop.

As she pumped herself up in the swing, she looked at the McCracken house, which she considered very stylish. Three dormer windows extending from its rust-streaked metal roof made it different from a plain, pointed-roof house, the kind that Walter drew. She had been trying to teach him how to draw a house with dormer windows, but it wasn't easy.

She was glad that her home was more than a house, that they had a farm, too. McCrackens didn't have to live out of a paper sack, running to the store all the time. The fenced garden was located on the south side of the house, where the sun warmed it in early spring. Turnips, cabbage, and butter beans would grow there until frost. The chicken house and run were nearby, so the tubs of chicken manure they used for fertilizer didn't have to be carried far. The whole south side of the chicken house was a big window to let the sun pour in and keep the hens warm and laying all winter.

Orchards were different. They belonged on the north. Maureen could see only one row of trees at the top of the north slope below the barn and the pigpens. Winter snow would melt there last, and the apple trees wouldn't bloom until spring had really come.

The loft under the spreading tin roof of the barn was crammed with hay. This time of year, in fall, no daylight showed through the hayloft, which was a good thing. Maureen could see cracks of light, however, between the thick, gray boards of the lower part of the barn where there were stalls for Fox and Jack, the mule team, and Molly, the milk cow.

The lane up from the cornfield and from Lost Creek separated the house yard from the barnyard, and fainter wagon traces led to the three fields east of the house. The one next to the barn lot grew pasture for the stock. The middle ridge field was planted in corn, in case the bottom field was flooded out. Hay was cut three times a summer from the south field. Maureen had a special path across it and a place to crawl under the barbed-wire fence to get to Sansoucies' and visit her friend Rose.

The woods of cedars, oaks, walnut, and hickory-nut trees spread above the farm like a dark frame on a picture.

Maureen liked to swing and look at the whole place. The clustered buildings seemed to keep each other company.

"Maureen, get in here!" Mit yelled from the back door.

She slid out of the swing. She knew she had to go in and change her wet shoes.

2

Maureen waited until Dad was home and the family was eating supper to start her account of crossing the trestle. She saw that Mit only half listened; maybe her story needed more action.

"It was raining cats and dogs, pitchforks and saw-logs"—Maureen waved her arms—"and our plank foot-bridge was bucking around like an outlaw horse." She got up from the table to demonstrate.

"Maureen, sit down and be mannerly. You haven't been excused from the table," Mama reminded her.

Maureen slid back into her place opposite Dad and Mit. Though everybody said those two looked alike, said Mit was the spitting image, the very spit of Cleve McCracken, Maureen thought there was considerable difference. For one thing, Dad's hair was streaked with gray, although he said it had been coal black when he was a kid like Mit. Then there were those forehead wrinkles over Dad's gray eyes. Mit had gray eyes, too, but Maureen didn't think he'd ever have wrinkles.

17

Maureen wished folks said she looked like someone in her family, but they didn't. They just said she was an O'Neil, whatever that meant. Certainly it didn't mean her appearance. O'Neil had been Mama's name before she was married, but Maureen didn't look like her. Mama's wavy hair was the color of sorghum syrup. She complained that Maureen's black hair was straight as a mule's tail. Wisps of it were always getting into her eyes. Maureen thought her eyes were fine for seeing, but not much for looks. They were sort of green, not big and brown like Rose Sansoucie's eyes.

Mama said Maureen had always been long-legged as a newborn colt. Maureen didn't mind that, for she was a fast runner, always chosen first to play Wolf Over the Ridge or Prison Base. She wondered if long legs had anything to do with being an O'Neil.

"Mama, what does it mean to be an O'Neil?"

"Well, some were kings and some were ne'er-do-wells. My goodness, what a change of subject." Mama shivered a little.

"Are you cold, Mama?" Maureen asked.

"No, I'm still thinking about you kids crossing the railroad trestle. It makes me downright nervous. There must have been hard rains south of Dotzero. I didn't think the creek would come up so fast. I was out looking for mushrooms when the rain drove me inside, and there was a stack of *Capper's Weeklies* from all summer. So I got to reading this continued story. If I'd realized there was high water, I'd have tried to hitch up Fox and Jack and meet you with the wagon."

"No need for you to try to handle that team, Mama," Mit said. "We got over the trestle all right. I checked the block signal."

"Walter did fine and dandy," Maureen said, "except he thinks he's skinny as a case knife and might fall through."

"I'd say Walter is shaped more like one of those little round cedar trees in the upper pasture," Dad teased.

"Still and all, we need a bridge. I worry so about you kids crossing that trestle," Mama said. "So does Pat Ash, working down there at Dotzero depot."

"Need a lot of things. Bridge ought to be at the top of the list," Dad agreed. "Especially in these hills where we get fast runoffs."

After all the chores were done and the supper dishes cleared from the oilcloth-covered kitchen table, Mit and Maureen spread their school books out. Maureen tried to concentrate on her long-division problems, but none of them came out even, which discouraged her. Only when they came out even could she be sure they were correct.

She traced her pencil around the carving on the back of her kitchen chair. Was the design a tassel or a palm tree in a cyclone? She couldn't decide.

There was no carving on the bench against the wall

near the cookstove. Plain as a plank, it had been made by some jackleg country carpenter, according to Dad. *Capper's Weekly* papers and some books were stacked at one end of it. On the other side of the cookstove, the woodbox left just enough room for the door to the cellar to swing open. Maureen surveyed the kitchen—Mama's worktable, the tall cabinet, the coal-oil stove used only in summer but always smelling of kerosene. For her, it was a comforting room.

She decided to read aloud to Walter from Hurlbut's *Story of the Bible*, which lay on the bench. They both liked it, although she had to be careful about the pictures she showed him in that book. Walter hated one of an Israelite slave being beaten and had ripped it halfway out of the book.

Maureen settled Walter on the bench beside her and read about the man who found his lost sheep. Then she read about the woman who swept out her whole house looking for a lost coin.

"Rattle, rattle, rattle," Mit objected. "I've got to study a poem and know it by heart. Miss Huckstep thinks it's better to have poems in your head than money in the bank."

"Maureen, read to yourself," Mama ordered.

"Well, I would, but it wouldn't do Walter any good. He hasn't had most of these words, because Miss Huckstep thinks the second grade ought not to learn anything except the second-grade reader, and if I was to—"

"Maureen talking machine, you cause me all kinds of trouble. Look at this composition I wrote last night." Mit held up a paper spotted with red marks. "These are all places I should have spelled Depression with a capital *D*."

"It's not my fault Depression is so bad you have to spell it with a capital *D*," Maureen protested.

"I might have thought of it and looked it up in *Capper's Weekly* if you hadn't been talking a blue streak."

"Well, anyhow, Miss Huckstep gets some funny notions," Maureen went on. "Like today, when second grade colored the black cats they drew. She didn't put Walter's up over the blackboard; said he didn't make the color lines all go the same way. That made Walter feel bad. So I just went up to her desk and told her that it was a kitten just been licked by the mother cat, fur every whichway. And she told me to—"

"Stop, babbling brook!" Mit held his head. "See. Now you almost made me forget the letter we picked up." He took the wrinkled envelope from his pocket and handed it to Mama.

She opened it and moved closer to the lamp. Mama read aloud, "Dear Lillian and Family. I wish I could write you better news, but I guess the luck of the O'Neils is running low. I never saw things so bad as they are now in St. Louis. I was laid off last spring, didn't get a lick of work for three months. Now I have got temporary work in a box factory, but it won't be for long.

21

We can't do much to help ourselves here in the city. There's no space to grow a garden, not even a decent lettuce bed. City rents are high. Work or no work, the landlord comes on rent day expecting his money. I was wondering if we could bunk for a while in the old smokehouse there at the home place. I can still carpenter, or wood butcher, ha ha, and could put in a rough floor and some windows. Used to be good land on the railroad right-of-way where we could put in a crop of potatoes come St. Patrick's Day. And there ought to be enough coal fall off the engine tenders for winter fuel. I know your house is small but thought the annex, ha ha, might be available. With love from your brother Millard. P.S. Don't bother to worry Ma any about this."

"The old smokehouse!" Maureen exclaimed. "It's torn down."

"Everybody knows that, parrot," Mit mumbled.

Dad's gray eyes were troubled. "Nothing left but a grease spot where hams used to drip. Millard went off to the city years ago, when wages were good. Now he expects everything to be the same here."

Mama reread the letter to herself, then said, "Even if the building stood, it would be a hard row to hoe for Millard and Cora and that family—nine children, no stock, no tools. Fox and Jack are the only power around here except elbow grease. Millard's family is used to electricity now. Still, we have to do what we can." Mama folded and refolded the letter. "Cleve, how are we going to answer this letter?"

Mama seemed cold again, and Dad checked the cookstove. The supper fire was almost out. When he poked split wood into the stove, sparks shot up. "Man is born to trouble as the sparks fly upward," he quoted. "That was the preacher's text last Sunday. Sure is gospel truth."

Maureen could see one of Dad's black moods coming on. Sometimes they lasted a whole day, even two days. It was just awful when Dad got all out of heart and didn't talk to them. The best thing to do was to try to get him thinking about something interesting.

"Well, say, do you know what I found out today? I found it right in the geography book we have now in fifth grade. It's printed across the map of where we live here in Missouri. It says St. Francois Mountains. Did you know that, Dad? Did you? Did you know we lived in the St. Francois Mountains? Mountains with names, just like the Rocky Mountains or the Cascade Mountains or any of them? Did you know?"

Dad shook his head.

"Be still, Maureen." Mit spoke in a low voice. "Dad's got other things to think about, and so have I."

"I think it's pretty important to know where you live and that you live in the St. Francois Mountains. Did you know that, Mama?"

"Just old, hardscrabble south Missouri hills, far as I

know." Mama sighed. "Names don't make living here any easier in these times. Now be still, Maureen, and let me try to think what we could offer. Eleven. That's a lot of people."

"It's no wonder you didn't know you were living in the St. Francois Mountains. Miss Huckstep didn't know it either; never even told us. I had to go to her desk and show it to her on the map."

"Right during our civics class," Mit said.

"And why did Miss Huckstep call Maureen a cracker box?" Walter asked.

"Cracker box?" Mama looked puzzled; then she smiled. "She must have said chatterbox."

Dad chuckled. Walter's comment had headed off his black mood. Everybody was always ready to laugh at her, Maureen brooded. Even Walter, telling on her like that. Here she'd gone and got the mail, helped Walter over the trestle, tried to tell them all something interesting, and all they ever did was tell her to stop talking.

Maureen didn't say good-night to Walter when Number 41, his bedtime train, went by and Mama led him off upstairs. But soon after Mama came down and started to work on her letter, Maureen heard him call.

"Somebody! Somebody come!" Walter yelled.

Without a word, Maureen got the broom and started upstairs. She liked to have the broom for protection on the dark stairway and in the upstairs hall.

Mama had left the coal-oil lamp burning low in the

24

room Walter shared with Mit. Walter made a little lump under the covers of his single bed in the corner.

"Okay, Walter, is it in the closet again?"

"Yes." Walter uncovered his eyes.

A few minutes later Maureen was back downstairs, well satisfied with the job she had done. "I can drive that spook out better than anybody. Walter said so," she announced to the others.

"It's your fault it's there," Mit stated. "I've heard all those scary yarns you tell him."

"I just go up there and fling open the closet door, and I whack around like this." Maureen demonstrated beating with the broom. "And I say, 'Get out of here! Out! Out! Don't you ever come back to pester Walter Lee McCracken again. And if you do, you'll be sorry.' I looked over at Walter, and I could tell by his eyes that he wasn't scared anymore and was smiling. So I said, 'You know there's nothing there just like there wasn't last night,' and he said 'Yes, but I want it chased out anyhow.' And I said, 'Now, Walter, if you would just—"

"Blatherskite!" Mama tore a sheet from Mit's ink-paper tablet. "Blatherskite! You're right, Mit, a person can't think with Maureen's rattling. How can I write Millard a sensible answer?"

All at once Maureen felt very tired. Well, all right, she'd never talk to them again. Maybe then they'd be happy. That's what they wanted.

Wordlessly she went to her little room at the end of

the upstairs hall and got undressed. After she was in bed, she brooded on all the names they called her—talking machine, parrot, babbling brook, blatherskite.

At last Maureen fell into a troubled sleep and felt herself falling, falling into rushing muddy water. She awoke on the floor beside her bed, struggling in her quilts. Maureen started to cry out that she'd had that dream again, the one where she fell off the bridge, but then she remembered her plan. Instead, she untangled the quilts and climbed silently back into bed.

3

The next morning Maureen looked out her dormer window at the white fog that lay like a roll of soft cotton along Lost Creek. If the water had not run down yet, it would be a job to get Walter over the trestle.

In the kitchen Mama put a plate of fried salt pork and eggs on the table in front of Dad. Then she hurried to strain the pail of foaming milk that he'd brought in. Mit had already given Fox and Jack their oat measure and turned them out to pasture. Walter found the rubbers Mama insisted they wear to school. Through all, Maureen remained silent. Nobody noticed.

When they were ready to leave for school, Mama handed Mit a letter. "Get this in the morning mail. Maybe God should have broken my arm when I was writing last night, but I went ahead and told Millard if worst came to worst there in the city, they could move in here with us." She pointed to the row of pegs over the woodbox. "We might have to hang some of you kids on nails."

Maureen said not a word. She just nodded good-bye.

Mama was right; they needed the rubbers. Along the bank of Lost Creek the layer of mud covering the sand came up in sheets with each step. Walter's tracks were almost as big as Mit's. Clusters of torn leaves caught far up in the willows on the bank showed how high and swift the water had been.

The sun burned through the fog, and under their footbridge shallow water glided smoothly over clean gravel. Walter pointed to the sparkling stream. "Is it the same creek as yesterday?"

To Maureen, Lost Creek seemed like a person who had gotten over a tantrum and was trying to be extra nice. She started to share this observation. "Say, I was just thinking. . . ." Suddenly she stopped.

"Thinking what?" Walter asked.

"Nothing."

"We know it's nothing," Mit said, "but finish it anyhow."

Maureen glared at him and was glad to hear a train whistle for the Dotzero crossing. The freight came on with a roar, casting its shadow over them as it thundered across the trestle. Mit and Walter couldn't hear Maureen call off the names of the passing cars: Missouri Pacific, M K and T, Illinois Central, C and E I, Denver and Rio Grande, Missouri Pacific, Missouri Pacific, Frisco, Pennsylvania. She liked the names of the railroad companies. They were a regular geography lesson.

She was also glad to know that her voice still worked.

"I counted five fellows bumming rides on that freight," Walter said.

"Men riding freights are common as pig tracks. I counted six. You missed one, Walter. How many did you count, Maureen?" Mit asked.

She didn't answer that question or any of the others they pestered her with. She was strong, firm, quiet. Much as she wanted to tell Mrs. Stackhouse of the offer to Uncle Millard, she kept on the road to school while Mit ran off to mail Mama's letter. Still, it was hard to resist Walter when he took hold of her hand and implored her to tell him what was wrong.

Mit was back in no time, for he never stopped to be friendly to Mrs. Stackhouse. "Don't beg her to talk, Walter," he said gleefully, when he heard Walter's appeal. "Just be thankful old Reen Peen is not running off at the mouth. She was vaccinated with a phonograph needle. Reen Peen, Reen Peen, used to talk till her face got green." Delighted with his chant, Mit repeated it.

Maureen flung down her books and covered her ears, but Mit only chanted louder. Finally Walter helped her pick up the books, and they went on, with Mit tormenting her all the way. When they reached the edge of the Dotzero School playground, Maureen knew she had to stop him. The whole school would hear her own brother teasing her. They would all start calling her Reen Peen.

She scooped up a handful of mud from the roadside ditch and drew back her hand in warning. Mit danced around, yelling louder. Something grasped Maureen and shook her—it was her own anger—and the mud flew.

Mit dodged. It wasn't a good throw. Only a little mud spattered on his jacket. Maureen got the worst of it; her hand was a mess. First she tried to wipe it off on the wet grass, then on the skirt of her cotton dress.

That day at school was the longest Maureen had ever put in. Though she knew the answer to almost all of Miss Huckstep's questions to the fifth grade, she didn't raise her hand. She did turn in all her written work, hoping it would show Miss Huckstep how smart she really was. Several times she saw Miss Huckstep looking at her in a puzzled way, and Maureen just nodded when she asked her if she felt all right.

Maureen missed her friend Rose. If only she had been at school, Maureen could have talked to her a little at recess.

When the long, long day finally ended, Maureen didn't even go into the store to ask for mail. So far no one except Walter seemed to care one whit that she'd given up speaking. Mit raced ahead, prancing and whistling as if he had some great news to tell.

He had to wait, for there was company when they got home. At the yard gate, they recognized the old Durant sedan that belonged to Mrs. Wiley. She lived in Beaumont. Grandma lived in Beaumont too, and sometimes she rode along when Mrs. Wiley came to see about all the places she owned between Dotzero and Post Oak.

Maureen loved company. With anticipation, she hurried through the kitchen and across the hall to the sitting room, where Mama was serving cookies and coffee. A sharp-eyed woman in an ugly brown dress sat in the best rocker by the stand table. Mrs. Wiley always looked the same. Her thin gray hair was combed back so tight it was a wonder she could bat her piercing eyes.

Grandma sat in a straight chair by the door and kissed Walter and Maureen as they came in. She would have kissed Mit as well if he hadn't dodged.

Mrs. Wiley looked the children over. "Lillian, you've got your work cut out for you. Sister, there, how old are you?"

Maureen ducked her head shyly and didn't answer.

"What's the matter, Maureen? Cat got your tongue?" Grandma asked. That was something you said to a little bit of a kid. Maureen stuffed a sugar cookie in her mouth to keep from answering.

"I'm seven," Walter volunteered.

Mrs. Wiley turned her attention to Mit. "Now a boy that age, he'd eat like a threshing hand. Bottomless pit, trying to fill him up."

As if to prove her right, Mit took more than his share

of cookies and fled from the sitting room. Walter chased after him.

Maureen pulled a footstool into a corner, hoping she wouldn't be noticed. If she couldn't take part in the conversation, she could at least listen and observe.

Although Mrs. Wiley and Grandma had been friends a long time, they were not much alike. Grandma O'Neil wore flowery dresses with lace collars and kept her hair frizzed in a permanent. Mrs. Wiley, on the other hand, wasn't a bit stylish, even if she did live in a brick house in town. People said she was land poor. They said she was as close as the bark on a tree with money, held on to a dollar until the eagle screamed, still had every last cent and every last acre her husband left her.

Mrs. Wiley came out from Beaumont in summer to chase blackberry pickers off her land. All year she drove over back roads to collect cash rent from the tenants of the ramshackle houses on her lands. One of those houses, on the nearby Wiley place, was where the Sansoucies lived. Mrs. Wiley had just come from there.

"I allowed I could ford the creek today." Mrs. Wiley put her coffee cup down with a clatter. "I put up with it just as long as I could. They haven't paid me a cent, not one red cent, for a year, and the place is getting run down with that big family. How can I make repairs? You know that place is special to me, being the old home place of my husband's people. He'd turn over in his grave if I let it go to ruin."

"Sansoucies might have some pigs to sell later on," Mama ventured.

"I've heard about those pigs for a year," Mrs. Wiley stated flatly. "I know times are hard. Nobody knows that better than I do, with the taxes I have to pay on my land. But I'm going to keep it free and clear—Sansoucies or nobody can change me on that—so I had no choice except to tell them they had to move out, and right away."

Maureen was dismayed. Rose was her best friend and the only girl her own age she had to play with on their side of Lost Creek. She didn't know what she'd do without Rose, who was quiet and didn't mind how much a person talked.

Conversation in the sitting room drifted to the possible size of the Sansoucie store bill, the disgracefully low market price of hogs, the number of quarts of canned food in the cellar. Maureen kept thinking of Rose and of all the Sansoucies. No matter how often she went there, she was always treated like company.

When Grandma asked if they had heard from Uncle Millard, Maureen kept silent, although she could have added much to Mama's statement that times were hard in the city, just as they were in the sticks.

At their departure, Mama followed the visitors to the yard gate. Maureen was still waving vigorously at the Durant lurching down the lane when Mama returned to the porch. She put her hands on her hips. "Well,

Maureen, I never! Young lady, I've got some hash to settle with you. I was so outdone! You know Grandma is getting hard of hearing. Out there at the gate, what do you think I heard Mrs. Wiley holler at her?" Mama popped out her eyes, turned down her mouth, and spoke in a harsh voice, imitating Mrs. Wiley. " 'Now that middle one, the girl, is she right bright? Didn't appear to be.' "

Maureen was silent. "You can't blame her," Mama declared. "You come in with your school dress as muddy as if you'd fallen in the pigpen, won't say how do or anything, and then just sit while we're visiting, listening with your mouth open fit to catch flies. I was just flabbergasted. Of course, your grandma stuck up for you, said you were sharp as a tack most of the time, a regular blatherskite. But, still, I felt ashamed of one of my own young ones."

Maureen broke away and raced across the yard to the tire swing. She didn't feel very good either. Her good friend would have to move away. The plan to make her family appreciate her wasn't working very well. Her silence suited Mit fine. But it bothered Walter, who didn't understand it, and it had made Mama ashamed of her.

Maureen went over these injustices as she swung back and forth. One thing sure, she wasn't going to give up. She'd make her family sorry they were mean

34

to her and called her names. At least, today had been different in one way. Other visits she'd been bawled out after company left for getting wound up, talking too much, and showing off.

4

By Saturday morning Maureen had such a tight feeling in her chest that she felt as if she were about to explode. She hoped her voice was still working, although she had learned from listening to Mit's hygiene class that muscles got weak and useless from lack of exercise.

After breakfast, the chances were that everyone would clear out and leave her alone in the kitchen. She sat down on the worn linoleum in front of the door that led to the cellar and waited. In the door's lower panel the wood grain formed a face. Maureen had named it Peloponnesus, a word she'd heard listening to Mit's geography class. When she had a chance, she would test her voice on Peloponnesus; she frequently talked things over with him.

Mit and Walter got instructions for the Saturday job Dad had given them. "There's a break in the upper side of the pasture fence by the sassafras tree," Dad had said. "Take your hammer and nails, some scrap wire, and mend it. Walter, you're straw boss on the job. I'll hitch up Fox and Jack to haul wood. When you finish, come help me load."

That took care of them. Mama said nothing could keep her in the house on such a sunny fall morning. She'd clean the hen house, the worst job on the place. It wouldn't seem so bad on such a good day.

As she took her barn jacket down from the peg near the cellar door, she stumbled over Maureen. "I declare, you'll cause me to fall and break a hip. Now if you can't help, don't hinder." Mama was never very definite about assigning chores.

As soon as the house was still, Maureen stared at the lower panel of the door. The distorted face in the wood was framed by lines that looked like long, flowing hair. "I have to tell you about Rose, Peloponnesus," she began. "She's going to have to move away, and I'll miss her and all the Sansoucies, miss them worse than payday. You don't find people like them every day. They treat company like family and family like company. But they're going, no two ways about it. I don't know when I'll ever again have a friend living right close, because we're here across Lost Creek.

"I've been thinking about a bridge and how you get one." Maureen nodded to Peloponnesus. "That's right. You know we need it. For a while there, it looked like we'd never get it, but then I just worked it out, and we'll soon have it. No more walking that trestle." Her voice was fine.

She talked for quite a while as she imagined the bridge with concrete sides, wide enough for two cars or wagons to pass, high enough for any flood. She told of all the families that would come across it to visit the McCrackens. They included everyone she knew in Dotzero and an imaginary family with girl triplets her own age.

"And I'll tell you something else, Peloponnesus," she continued. "Everybody in our family was just dumbbellfounded that I got us that bridge. Well, they said it was just like some kind of magic how I got it."

"Ah, ha! Dumbbellfounded!" Mit lunged across the kitchen and seized Maureen by the shoulders. "So you *can* talk! Even got us a bridge. Who were you talking to, Maureen?"

"Nobody."

"You're talking to yourself. Only crazy people talk to themselves."

Maureen tried to shake off his grip. "You're supposed to be fixing the fence."

"I forgot my nails here in the kitchen."

"Dummy, you only had to remember three things, and you forgot one," Maureen jeered.

"Well, this way I heard you got us a bridge." Mit shook her and shrieked with laughter.

Anger gripped Maureen, and she jabbed Mit in the stomach with her elbow. He let go of her shoulder. She beat at his face with both fists. Wham! Her head rang from a terrible, jarring slap.

Tears almost blinded Maureen as she grabbed Mit around the neck in what she hoped was a choking hold. "I've got you in a hammerlock," she said panting.

"Oh, no, you haven't, blatherskite bridge builder." He tried to shake her off the way Tisket shook a rat. She held on.

They struggled across the hall into the sitting room. Mit forced Maureen's head down onto the floor and held her there by the back of the neck. With his other arm across her back, he tried to flip her over. "A beautiful half nelson! A beauty!" he yelled.

"I'll break that hold," Maureen muttered. "I'll get you in a hammerlock." She gathered all her strength and came up. Mit came up too. His foot hit the little stand table. Crash! Over went the table and everything on it.

Mit and Maureen stood apart, staring at the damage. Mama's cut-glass dish lay in four pieces. Maureen picked up the biggest piece and held it helplessly. Uncle Millard had given Mama and Dad that dish for a wedding present.

Mama had left her rubber boots on the porch, so they didn't hear her coming. She appeared in the doorway in baggy overalls and her barn jacket. Her pretty hair was stuffed under Dad's old felt hat. Her face was smudged, and she smelled like the chicken house.

Although she was likely due for a switching, Maureen didn't think about herself for a second or so. She thought about Mama and how different she must have looked when Uncle Millard had given her that cut-glass dish.

"Can't I step out of this house for one minute?" Mama yelled. "I see the two of you managed to break just about the only nice thing I had."

"Mit started it. He jumped out at me and shook me around."

"Maureen jabbed me right in the gut, then tried to choke me to death."

"Clear out of here, both of you," Mama shrieked. "I don't want to hear any more."

"I wasn't doing one thing to him, Mama, wasn't even talking to him, and he comes and. . . ."

"Shut up, Maureen," Mama said with a sob. "Shut up and leave me alone for a while."

Maureen fled to the tire swing. She watched Mit as he started off, swinging his hammer as if nothing had happened. The accident was all his fault, too. He'd started it, but Mama wouldn't listen to her. Mama had told her to shut up, first time she'd spoken for two days.

Maureen's head touched the side of the tire, and her ear felt sore. That was from Mit's slap. She remembered a story his class had read about Thomas A. Edison, who went deaf after he was slapped.

If she went deaf, Mit would be sorry. They'd all be sorry. She listened to a train whistling far off for the Dotzero crossing. Did it sound fainter than usual? Making her deaf would be one awful thing for Mit to have on his conscience, even for a little while.

5

Maureen braced her feet in the bare spot under the swing to give herself a push. Nobody had given her a job. Mama wanted to be left alone. Walter didn't need her. He was getting to be like Mit, too big for his britches, fixing fence and loading wood. Tisket was off chasing rabbits.

Maureen heard faint, faraway shouts. The Sansoucie kids were playing. She wouldn't hear that much longer. She'd better get over there and play while she had a chance. Saturday had started wrong, but there was no use in wasting the rest of it.

Without asking permission, Maureen slipped out the yard gate to her path through the hayfield. When she got to the Wiley place, her cotton stockings and dress hem were itchy with sticktights. But she had no time to pick off the hitchhiking burrs; they would have to wear off. The Sansoucies were playing a game of Prison Base with much yelling.

"Rose, Rose," Maureen called. "I've come to play."

Rose swung a toddler onto her hip and left the game to come greet Maureen. Though Rose was small for her age, she could do something Maureen couldn't do. She could run and carry a little kid at the same time. Of course, the kids were trained to hang on. That helped.

"Maureen, I'm proud you came early." It was nice to see Rose's big smile. "I've finished my Saturday work, much as we can do in our house. Nothing to do now but mind the least ones. You got done early too, huh?"

"I was going to help all day long, but Mit caused Mama's cut-glass dish to get broken."

Rose sucked in her breath. "Oh, that was so pretty."

"I didn't like it much, looked like cat scratches to me, but Mama liked it. And she just broke up, worse than the dish, and told me to shut up before I had a chance to say anything. And Mit smartin' out all the time, so I thought I'd come over here." She studied her friend for a moment. "Rose, you look different."

Rose smoothed her hair. "Mom gave us all haircuts. She said she didn't want us looking like bur-oak acorns when we went anywhere. Do you think she botched the job?"

Rose's hair looked as if it had been cut with a knife and fork. "It'll grow out," Maureen said.

The other children motioned and called to the two girls.

"If you want to play Prison Base, you can be on my side." Rose shifted the little one to her other hip. "I

43

get an extra player because I have to pack this one. Or would you want to get the little ones together and play house?"

"Prison Base!" Maureen raced toward Rose's team. The more running and shouting, the better Maureen liked the game.

Afterward they played Wolf Over the Ridge, Rotten Egg, and Lemonade. Then Rose suggested Antony Over. The low Wiley house was just right to throw a ball over the roof for the team on the opposite side to catch. They played until the ball rolled down the roof and lodged in the rusting roof gutter.

Maureen knew she shouldn't stay to eat at noon. There was little enough of the cold biscuits and mashed turnips for the Sansoucies. But they invited her politely and even opened a quart of canned blackberries because she was company.

After dinner the little kids took naps, and Maureen and Rose had a chance to hunt hickory nuts without having to drag babies along.

Finally, in late afternoon, Maureen knew she had to go back across the meadow. It had been so pleasant talking to Rose as they searched among the big, golden hickory leaves that Maureen had almost forgotten the misery of the morning. She felt her ear; it was still sore. She wondered what Mama would say about her being gone all day. Whatever it would be, Maureen decided not to hear very well, if at all.

44

As Maureen came to the back porch, Mama raised the shade on the kitchen-door window. "Now where have you been, Maureen? I called and called you to come take your bath right after Walter. We've all had ours. You'll have to have yours later in fourth water."

Everybody was in the kitchen. There was hardly room for the washtub that was pushed near the stove. Maureen preferred a switching to a bath in that cold, gray water, so she decided to ignore Mama's order.

Mama looked like a different person with clean clothes and just-washed hair. She started to peel potatoes. "I hope nobody faints from hunger before I get supper on the table. I'm late starting, but I had a lot to do outside and could have used some help from Maureen. Even so, I stayed out as long as I could. Took a walk over by the Wiley cemetery. You know that rose of Sharon bush there? I picked a bouquet for the stand table so it wouldn't look so bare." She didn't look at Maureen.

"Funny thing about that bush," Dad said. "Without fail, it blooms every fall. Money runs out, people go broke, stand in breadlines. Old Hitler and old Mussolini take over across the water. The whole world changes, and that bush blooms just the same."

Mama nodded. "That's a good thing for you to remember, Cleve, when you get down-in-the-mouth."

Mit's face was soap shined, and his wet black hair was combed back in a pompadour. "Maureen, you didn't tell us where you were. You sure made yourself scarce. We needed you to open field gates when we hauled wood."

"What?"

"Where were you this afternoon when we needed you?"

"What?"

"What, what, stick your nose in a coffeepot. Pull it out when it gets red hot," Mit chanted.

So far Mit wasn't overly concerned that she couldn't hear thunder. Walter began to pester her with questions she didn't answer. He finally gave up and announced that Maureen was now both deef and dumb. Nobody thought one thing about it except to laugh because Walter said *deef* instead of *deaf*.

At supper Maureen had to listen to Dad and Mit brag about what a help Walter had been. Walter smiled until his eyes shut. After she'd finished eating, Maureen got right up from the table and started stacking dishes.

"I'm glad to see you're going to do dishes without a fuss," Mama said. "Be sure to fasten the chicken-house door when you pitch out the dishwater. Did you hear me?" she asked in an exasperated voice.

Maureen didn't answer; she stared blankly at Mama.

"What's the matter with you, Maureen?" Mama demanded. "I cleaned the chicken house by myself, not one lick of help from you. You had enough pep, though, to break my bowl. Now the least you can do is see that all the chickens have gone to roost and then fasten the door."

There were a lot of dishes and pans for just five people. It was dark when Maureen finished, and she went to bed without taking a bath.

When she came downstairs the next morning, she knew something was wrong. In the kitchen, Mama was tight-lipped and unsmiling.

Dad called from the back porch, "The waste of it, to see a young laying hen mauled like this. She was just full of eggs, Lillian. Come look at this." Maureen followed Mama outside. Dad pulled a cluster of little yellow spheres from inside the back of a hen. "I'll dress this one. The other two were so mutilated there's no use to try to dress them to cook. Total loss." He looked up at Maureen. "When I went to turn the chickens out, I found them up in the plum trees around the yard. Three hens were dead inside the open door of the chicken house. A 'possum or weasel got them."

"You didn't mind last night, Maureen. I told you to shut the door. Why didn't you?" Mama asked. "Why can't you take some responsibility, be dependable?"

Maureen took a deep breath. "I was going to, to do something for all of us, responsible like, and I was just thinking about it and how I could do it and all, and sometimes I can't figure out how anything is going to work unless I talk about it, and when I talk everybody tells me to shut up all the time. So I wasn't bothering

47

anybody, just kind of thinking out loud, and like I tried to tell you, along comes Mit, and he starts tormenting me and aggravating me and he gets me so mad. Then he lams me up the side of the head, kerwhack. He hit me so hard that my head rang just like a bell. And I saw stars and I couldn't hear very well, only nobody would listen to me if I tried to tell them. All day yesterday I couldn't hear very well on account of this busted eardrum or whatever it is, and so when you said that to me last night, I couldn't hear you for sure, and. . . ."

Maureen stopped talking. Mama's lips were moving; she was saying something. Maureen couldn't hear one word. A scared feeling grew in her stomach like an expanding balloon. What was Mama saying? She couldn't hear!

Then came the far-off sound of the Sansoucies shouting at play. Tisket barked; a train whistled. From the top of the stairs Walter called, "Maureen, come help me find my Sunday shirt."

Maureen sighed with relief.

"I see you haven't learned to read lips yet." Mama still looked stern. She didn't say anything about a switching. Maybe she couldn't think of any punishment bad enough to pay for killing three laying hens.

Maureen thought over her deaf act. It sure had been a dumbbell thing to pretend. Even if she were really deaf, she would want her family to be proud of her, not sorry. Now she had to prove that she could be a dependable, responsible middle kid, the kind Mama wanted. She'd start with the hens.

"I'll pay you back for the hens, Mama."

"I won't hold my breath," Mama said.

6

Monday morning Maureen was surprised and pleased when the Sansoucie children came trooping across the meadow to join the McCrackens for the walk to school.

Maureen stayed close to Rose as they crossed the footbridge. "I hope you come all week," she said. "We're going to have a spelling match and a ciphering match on Friday."

"Only coming today," Rose said in her gentle, low voice.

"Don't worry when you see your desk is empty," Maureen assured her. "I took your pencil, your tablet, and your box of colors and put them in my desk so nobody would steal your pink crayon. Pink, that's the one they either steal or borrow and use up."

"Much obliged for taking care of my things. I'll soon get them out of your way." Rose stopped to let the other children go ahead. "I hate to tell you this, but we're going to move. We came to school today to get stuff from our desks and to tell Miss Huckstep good-bye. My dad found a place in Cold Spring school district. We can live in the tenant house, and he'll get some work from the farmer that owns it."

"Mrs. Wiley is the meanest person I know, and I know a lot of mean people," Maureen stated angrily.

Rose shrugged. "We've got nothing against her. We might be better off at Cold Spring. My mom says she can't do anything to make the Wiley house pretty. She papered the walls with clean newspaper, but it didn't help much. Still, I'd like to stay here where Miss Huckstep is teacher. I had aimed to come to school regularly whenever we could get across the creek. I won't have any friend at Cold Spring."

"How about me?" Maureen asked with self-pity. "You'll have enough kids around for lots of good games, but I won't. After you move, I can't jump wide rope unless I tie one end of the rope to a post and beg Walter to turn the other. I can't depend on Mit for anything except torment."

During recess Maureen stayed close to Rose, and at noon they took the tin lard buckets that held their lunches and went to eat at the edge of the playground. Maureen couldn't help but see that Rose had only two biscuits that were not even buttered, just stained with a little berry jelly.

She offered Rose part of her chicken sandwich, explaining that McCrackens had an extra lot of chicken due to a sort of accident. Rose said she didn't like chicken. Maureen knew that couldn't be, and finally she talked her into taking some.

At four o'clock, when the school day was done, Miss Huckstep had cards prepared showing what grades the Sansoucie children were in. "Give these to the teacher at Cold Spring School," she said, as she handed Rose the cards. "Enroll right away, and be sure to go to school every day."

"Yes ma'am," Rose said politely.

The two girls went together down the hill to the store, but Rose waited on the porch while Maureen went in to the postal window.

"We got *Capper's Weekly*." Maureen held up the newspaper when she came out. "No letter, though. I was expecting mail from Uncle Millard. Mama wrote and told him the family could live with us if the box factory closed down. Must be still going. Don't you want to ask for mail, Rose? You never know what you might get. All you have to say is 'Any mail for Sansoucie?'"

Rose shook her head. "My dad said for us not to go into the Stackhouse store."

"Why?"

"Last time my dad was in there to do some trading, Mr. Stackhouse was right overbearing."

It was Saturday before Maureen saw the Sansoucies again. She had just thrown kitchen scraps out to the chickens when she saw the whole Sansoucie family coming across the field. With long strides she ran to meet Rose, who walked ahead of the rest.

"Maureen, we've all come to tell you folks good-bye." Rose gestured back to the other children and to her parents who carried the smallest ones. "But I wanted to be first to ask you to come visit us at Cold Spring whenever you can."

"Oh, I will," Maureen promised. "It's not very far. And maybe you can come stay all night with me some-time. There's plenty of room until Uncle Millard, Aunt Cora, and all my cousins come."

Mr. Sansoucie came up and held out his hand to Maureen. "Sure looked natural, you galloping across that meadow, Maureen. We're much obliged to you for being company to our kids." He shook her hand just as if she were grown up.

Dad had described Mr. Sansoucie as wiry, and Maureen agreed. She felt he could be bent every whichway and not break. Rose's mother wouldn't break either. She was too soft. Her voice, her flesh, her handshake were all soft. She tried hard to make soft things that looked pretty.

"Mom, can we give Maureen her keepsake present now?" Rose asked.

"We made two, one for you and one for your mother," Mrs. Sansoucie said, as she handed Maureen folded cloths. "It's new goods of a chick-feed sack, the last bag we bought. Rose hemmed them, and I crocheted trim for the ends to make fancy hand towels. Or dresser scarves, if you want to use them for that."

"Oh, they're nice. Thanks a lot. I never had a keepsake present before."

"I see your dad and mom out by the lot gate," Mr. Sansoucie said. "I better get up there for the last of my borrowing from the McCrackens. We can't move unless we borrow Fox and Jack and the wagon."

Mrs. Sansoucie gave Mama her present, and Mr. Sansoucie told Dad how much obliged they were for all the McCrackens' help. Then he asked to borrow the team and wagon.

"You're welcome to them," Dad said, "but I'd better drive the mules across the ford when you're ready. There are some washed-out holes there, but I know where the water is shallow and the gravel firm."

"It'll be mighty lonesome over here on this side of the creek with you folks gone," Mama said. "Maureen and Walter won't have any children to play with. Of course, Mit is getting up now to where he doesn't have much time for play. It's easy to learn to play, harder to learn to work, I've found. Mit's a lot of help to Cleve."

"We'll miss good neighbors," Mr. Sansoucie said, "but we never cared much for the Wiley place. The chimney is so unhandy. It takes too much pipe to set up a heating stove."

In late afternoon all the Sansoucies, in the wagon

loaded with furniture, stopped at McCrackens'. As Dad drove off toward the ford, Maureen and Walter waved and waved, the way they waved at passenger trains.

"There go all my friends in one wagon, Walter." Maureen had finally stopped waving, and she had an empty feeling. "Maybe we ought to go over to the Wiley place and see how it is with everyone gone."

They set off across the meadow with Tisket following. The Wiley place looked so lonesome that Tisket whined at the sight. Maureen and Walter skirted the sagging yard fence where hummocks of dry grass and weeds from bygone summers had made the ground uneven. With an awful squawk, something flapped up, just missing their faces. Walter almost fell into a nest full of eggs.

"Sansoucies missed one of their hens. No wonder, she's hidden her nest. And she's off schedule, too, setting in the fall," Maureen said. "You never can tell about a Rhode Island Red."

While the hen clucked and fussed nearby, Walter touched one of the warm eggs. He asked about the nesting habits of various birds and fowl—guineas, geese, penguins.

"Walter, everything that has wings lays eggs," Maureen asserted blithely.

"Do angels lay eggs?"

Maureen looked at him sharply. "Walter Lee Mc-Cracken, you just better watch out, asking things like

55

that." Still, she pondered the question. Maybe Hurl-but's *Story of the Bible* might tell. Or she could talk it over with Peloponnesus.

The children cupped their hands around their eyes and looked through the windows into the small, vacant rooms. Most of the walls were covered with yellowed newspaper. "That's where their stove was, and over in that corner is where we played school on rainy days." Maureen moved to another window. "Somehow this house doesn't seem empty," she said.

She ran across the bare yard to the cistern pump and gave the handle a turn. "Look, they left this. I heard Mrs. Wiley say, like as not, they would take everything that wasn't nailed down. This is kind of loose, so watch out." She turned the handle until water splashed out from the pump spout. *"Helen, Helen, Helen.* That's what cistern pumps say, don't you think, Walter?"

A tall metal case covered the pump wheel and its chain with the little copper cups that brought water up from the cistern. A lid like an old-time soldier's hat fit on top of the case. Maureen pried it off and looked down into the black shaft. The wheel and cups took up most of the space, but the water below mirrored a bit of the sky. Her own head was reflected in the water, and something else floated there too.

"Walter," she called, "you won't believe what I've found. Just what you were asking about. An angel's egg. They lay their eggs in water, like frogs do, you

56

know, and there's one here in the Wiley place cistern. Want to see it?"

Walter's eyes came just to the top of the pump case. "You're an awful chunk," Maureen said, as she strained to lift him so he could see down the cistern shaft. "If we had asked Peloponnesus, he could have told us where to find it. But I guess we managed to find it by ourselves."

Walter saw the reflection of Maureen's head and part of his own. Then he saw a bright sphere floating. Maureen jiggled the pump handle. Far down in the cistern the metal cups on their chain moved. So did the sphere.

"That's a ball, Maureen, a red rubber ball." Walter's voice echoed in the cistern. "Red rubber ball, red rubber ball," he shouted in order to hear the echo.

Maureen dropped him with a jolt. "You're the one wanted to know about an angel's egg. I find you one. Now you won't believe it."

"Would so, too, if you found me a real one, but I know that's a ball. Sansoucies had a red one. Somehow it got into the cistern."

Maureen thought of the Antony Over game when the ball had stuck in the roof gutter. Rain might have washed it into the downspout, which led into the cistern. Still, it was interesting to think it could be an angel's egg.

"Now, Walter," she said, "there are a lot of wonderful things going on in the world, and I don't want you to miss any. You will if you decide that something that could be wonderful is just an old rubber ball, so once in a while. . . ."

"Maureen, Mit says a lot of the stuff you tell me is just malarkey, that you should go tell it to the Marines. Mit says you are the worst blatherskite—"

"Mit says! If he knows so much, you can just go and tag along after him and get him to chase things that aren't there out of your closet at night." Maureen turned and stomped off across the yard. At the broken gate she glanced back. Walter looked very small beside the vacant house. But he knew his way home. He had to learn that she wouldn't put up with any old thing. He was getting more and more like Mit and wouldn't listen.

Now she had no one at all. Maureen sniffed back tears. After a while she began to go over the names and ages of the departed Sansoucies. Then she talked to herself about a still larger imaginary family. As she wandered along the edge of the meadow, she gave them all names and ages. When there was any trouble, they could all depend on the middle child, a girl Maureen's age who was most reliable.

By the time she reached home Maureen felt better. Smoke drifted from the chimney, which meant that Mama had started the supper fire and would nab her and make her help if she wasn't careful. Then Maureen remembered the hen and the hidden nest. She burst into the kitchen, ready to tell Mama about the discovery.

Mama was rolling out biscuit dough. "Maureen, you didn't ask to go over to that empty house. Walter has been home for a long time. He had to come alone. You should not have left him over there by himself, playing around that old cistern. He could have been snakebit around the house foundation or run a rusty nail into his foot."

"But he didn't, and anyhow Tisket was with him, Mama."

"I never thought you would go back on Walter." Mama shook her head.

"I didn't. He got smarty over at the Wiley place, where it's just so lonesome. If you find an old rag or worn-out shoe or anything, it makes you feel like bawling because you knew them and don't know when you will ever see them again or have anybody to play with besides Walter. Anyhow, I'm dependable about replacing those hens. I've got one, and when the chicks hatch out, won't be any time until I'll have the other two, even have two to spare."

Mama put her hands on the sides of her head, flattening her pretty hair. "What *are* you talking about?" she asked.

"I've got to get some corn and take it back over there for this old biddy hen the Sansoucies left. She hid her nest outside the chicken house and has four eggs. I'll coax her into a basket with corn and bring her and the eggs here and put them in the hen house so the varmints won't get them. Then I'll take care of them and raise them."

"It's a wonder that hen didn't come out of the brush and flop down to have her legs tied, the Sansoucies move so often," Mama said. "You know she belongs to them, and you know the story about counting unhatched chicks. When a hen gets broody in the fall, she goes into a late molt, runs around half feathered, stuffs on corn all winter, and won't lay until spring. Still, the Sansoucies ought to have her." Mama looked out the kitchen window. "There will still be daylight after supper. I'd like to walk over to the Wiley place myself. You can't manage a setting hen alone."

Mama was worse than Walter. If there was something you wanted to skip over, not think about, she wouldn't let you leave it out. Maureen knew Mama was right that the hen and chicks to come weren't McCrackens'. There went her scheme to be responsible and replace their lost chickens. Still, she thought, brightening, if she helped the real owners get them back, that was an even better kind of responsible.

7

At school a few days later Maureen announced that all four eggs had hatched. Miss Huckstep seemed so interested that Maureen started to repeat the story of the hidden nest.

"We understand, so you need not tell it again," Miss Huckstep interrupted. "If you want to surprise the Sansoucies with their poultry, I'll take you over there Saturday. I've wondered if they enrolled in Cold Spring School."

Maureen hadn't expected to see the Sansoucies again for a long time. It just showed what good luck came from stepping carefully on the stones of the shortcut path. Maureen reminded Walter of this as they waited for Miss Huckstep to arrive in the Huckstep family Model A Ford.

Miss Huckstep knew just how to ease a car into Lost Creek ford: slowly enough to keep the coils dry, then quickly down on the gas, to keep from miring in the loose gravel. Maureen and Walter sat squeezed on the

61

front seat beside her, holding a basket of peeping baby chicks across their laps. The mother hen had put up a squawking fight, but now lay quietly at their feet with her legs tied together. On the back seat lay a bag of wheat and a bag of cracked corn for the chicks. Mama had sent squash, potatoes, and onions for the Sansoucies.

"We're much obliged to you for taking us, Miss Huckstep," Maureen said. "I think I could walk it, but not with an old Rhode Island Red about to flog me with every step. I don't know about Walter. His legs aren't as long as mine. By rights, he ought to come, though. He helped find the nest."

Miss Huckstep checked the block signal and crossed the railroad track at Cold Spring. After they passed the school, they rode by a farmhouse with a big barn. The tenant house would be close to it.

As they steered around a thicket matted with honeysuckle vines they saw the place. Rose and her sisters were hanging wash on the line, and they seemed like familiar movie stars in a new picture show. When the car stopped, the Sansoucie children were startled and started to run inside.

Maureen jumped out. "It's me, Rose. I promised I'd come visit."

"Maureen! You've come already." Rose smiled. "You kids go tell the folks Miss Huckstep is here."

"We've brought you a present," Maureen said lifting the hen out of the car.

The visitors were soon surrounded by all the Sansoucies, who thought their hen had been carried off by a fox.

"Leave it to Maureen to get here to see us and bring extra, besides," Mrs. Sansoucie said. Maureen could see the tenant house had many handy things, including a proper hen coop, where the Rhode Island Red was soon scratching and clucking to her brood. "She'll feel at home in no time, the way we did. You folks come in and see our place," Mrs. Sansoucie invited.

Maureen looked at the low house, which seemed to be held up by a huge trumpet creeper vine that grew to the roof. The surrounding sheds appeared even more interesting. Much as she liked to visit, she decided to stay outside.

"There must be great places to hide for I Spy," she said to Rose.

"Best of any place we ever lived," Rose assured her. "So we can play that to start. I'll be It. Remember, you're not playing, Bud." She spoke to a glum-looking boy sitting by the woodpile.

"Why can't he play, Rose?"

"He's not to run and rip and wear out his shoes in case we go to school."

There were so many good games to play, and later on so many places to explore with Rose, that Maureen did not go inside at all while Miss Huckstep talked with Mr. and Mrs. Sansoucie. The visit was over too soon.

"There's lots more to show you. When are you coming again?" Rose asked.

"Some of these days. You never can tell about Walter and me. At least, I know you're not gone for good now. I'll think of you over here, yelling and playing and wearing out the grass in another yard."

Rose's brown eyes were serious. "I think finding our hen was a good sign."

"Well, yes, and how about Miss Huckstep bringing us here on her Saturday? She's an extra good teacher."

"I know," Rose agreed. "She's better than most."

The road to Cold Spring was so narrow that Miss Huckstep pulled far to the side when they met another car. "I'm glad you kids had the chickens to take. We'll have to think of some other reasons for visits. I don't believe I got very far with my urging."

"We'd like to come anytime, wouldn't we, Walter? Maybe after Mama gets every last thing all canned, jellied, pickled, squeezed out, dried, she'll come too. She likes to get away from home, get a change of scenery. What would we be urging?"

Miss Huckstep laughed. "If you'd let me get a word in edgewise, I'll tell you. I'm trying to get the Sansoucies to go to school. They haven't started, and it's a downright shame. They're smart."

"Especially Rose," Maureen agreed.

"You have to keep right after them to get them to go

to school. I wasn't doing very well myself at Dotzero."
Miss Huckstep steered to miss a deep rut. "Cold Spring
is worse. The teacher is Lorene Stackhouse."

"Stackhouse!" Maureen exclaimed.

"Yes. Sterling Price Stackhouse is her uncle. She was
in my high-school class, and she was the last one of us
hired to teach a school. I just have my doubts that the
Sansoucies will set foot in a school taught by a Stackhouse. Of course, you might be able to talk them into
it, Maureen."

"Well, I'll try, but sometimes my folks claim I talk
too much," Maureen admitted.

Miss Huckstep reached over and gave her a pat.
"You'll have to learn to use that gift of gab the right
way."

All during the next week, Maureen was anxious to
stop at the post office and tell Mrs. Stackhouse about
her visit to Cold Spring, but Mit dashed in ahead of her
every day and asked for their mail. Finally she had a
chance the day Mit stayed home from school to help
Dad haul corn. Besides asking for mail, she had to get
a box of salt for Mama.

"Are you sure that's all?" Mrs. Stackhouse asked, as
she added the item to the McCracken bill.

" 'Tis for now. Even with Walter to help pack, I
can't carry too much across our footbridge. Might lose
my balance. Mama will be coming in to get a lot of

65

things." Maureen looked across at the dry-goods side of the store. "She'll be getting dress goods and a lot of stuff. She could hitch up Fox and Jack and come in the wagon, but she says she'd rather be in hell with her back broke than try to handle that stubborn pair.

"She claims Mit hasn't got the patience to drive them. They mind my dad, but he's either working on the railroad extra gang, which is lucky, or, if he doesn't have work, he's hauling corn for Fox and Jack. And then he says mules are like people, ought to have a day of rest once a week. But sometimes it doesn't make much sense to me. We have Fox and Jack so we can plant corn and cut hay. And we have to grow corn and hay to winter Fox and Jack. So. . . ."

"Whoa, Maureen, back up a little. I want to know about the Sansoucies. You said you visited them at Cold Spring. So they've moved away from Dotzero?"

"Oh, yes, they were asked to move, because Mrs. Wiley wanted cash rent. I told Rose I thought Mrs. Wiley was mean, but I never let on to any of 'em that I knew they had to move. Rose didn't say anything, so I didn't either. Never opened my mouth about it because I thought, well, might make 'em feel bad."

"I wouldn't worry about their tender feelings. They've got enough gall." Mrs. Stackhouse raised her voice. "Sterling, it's just the way we thought. They moved without a word about their store bill."

Mr. Stackhouse brought an account pad to the counter. He pushed his felt hat back on his head and adjusted his glasses the better to read the figures. "You can't get blood out of a turnip, and a good bit of it is my fault. I let this run on too long. But when them little peaked-faced young uns come in here with their dad, I just weighed up a few more beans."

"Yes, you should have shut them off before you did. We've got our own bills to think about," Mrs. Stackhouse said.

"Walter and I would never have got over there with that old hen if it hadn't been for Miss Huckstep. The Sansoucies left a hen, only there were five chickens when we went, because Miss Huckstep. . . ."

"Miss Huckstep, now how is she anyhow?" Mrs. Stackhouse seemed especially interested. "How is her term of school going?"

"Tol'able I guess. We're going to have a ciphering match every Friday. Miss Huckstep says the kids in eighth grade will pass their final examination if they come to school regular."

"Well, I declare." Mrs. Stackhouse puffed heavily from climbing up on the store step stool. "I guess Alma Huckstep is a born teacher. Like as not, she'll be an old maid."

"No, she won't." Maureen was emphatic.

Mr. Stackhouse chuckled. "Can't never tell for sure."

"Yes, you can so too. About her anyhow."

Mrs. Stackhouse reached high to arrange cans on a

shelf. "I know she's been going with Jim Nolan, the carrier on Dotzero rural route. But that could go on for a long time. He's got a mother to keep house for him. I've asked him about Alma, but I can't get a word out of him. Alma Huckstep could wait around for him and end up an old maid."

Maureen was pleased to have news. "No, she won't, because they are married already. Secretly married."

"Are they now?" Mrs. Stackhouse purred. "I wouldn't be too sure of that if I were you, Maureen."

"I saw it printed out, right in the St. Louis paper, little bitty print. I was at the Sansoucies' when they lived at the Wiley place where they had papered their kitchen with newspapers. One day we were playing school and didn't have any books. I was teacher, and I gave one of the kids the big print to read. He was slow, so while he was stumbling around reading that big print from the newspaper on the wall, I read the little print under marriage licenses, and I saw it. I told Mama about it."

"And what did she say?" Mrs. Stackhouse purred another question.

"She said if Miss Huckstep never said anything about getting married, then as far as she knew, there wasn't anything to it, and for me just to be still and forget about it."

"In that case, I guess you're right. Alma won't be

68

an old maid." Mrs. Stackhouse seemed very pleased, considering she wasn't even kin to Miss Huckstep.

Maureen felt important. Both Mr. and Mrs. Stackhouse were paying attention to what she had to say. It was a good opportunity to ask Mr. Stackhouse something she had wondered about. "There are lots of bridges over creeks and rivers. Almost every place has a bridge. Why don't we have one over Lost Creek for a wagon or a car so we can go places even if it rains?"

"Who's up there, Maureen, on the other side of Lost Creek, except you folks and the hoot owls? Even the Sansoucies loaded up and pulled out. Just not enough people up there in your neck of the woods."

As business was slack, Maureen stayed and chatted for a long time with Mr. and Mrs. Stackhouse. It sure would be nice to have a mother and father like them who really listened, she thought. Finally Walter got so fidgety that Maureen had to tear herself away and go home.

8

Maureen came home full of talk and was glad when Dad and Mit finished their chores and joined the family in the kitchen. Mama had just started supper.

"I thought we would never get out of that store," Maureen reported, "because there were Mrs. Stackhouse and Mr. Stackhouse acting like they were downright lonesome, wanting to know about everything."

"Sterling Price Stackhouse must know where he can get information." Mama put the biscuits in the oven.

"Price? Why does he have that name?" Walter asked. "Is Price his maiden name?"

Walter was puzzled when everyone laughed, so Maureen had to explain. "Of course not. He was named after General Sterling Price. That was a general in Missouri in the Civil War. I learned that from Mit's history class. His nickname was Pap. Pap Price, that's what they called him. Once I heard men talking on the store porch about when Pap Price and Abe Lincoln had their war, like there were only two people in the war."

70

"You're getting off the track," Mama reminded her. "You were telling us about all the attention you got at the store today."

Maureen felt wonderful. She was getting attention at home, too. "Yes, they told me the sawmill might shut down and some people move from Dotzero. And they asked me again about Uncle Millard and how his family was getting along. I told them they were having it hard, couldn't have a cow or chickens or anything there in the city, and that Mama had written and told them they could crowd in with us."

"That's family business. You don't need to advertise it." A gloomy look came over Dad's face.

"Appears Stackhouses were uncommon nosey even for them," Mama said. "Didn't they give you any news?"

"Yes, they said the Sansoucies moved and left a big store bill."

Dad sighed. "Not much news in that."

Maureen thought for a second. "And Mr. Stackhouse thinks we don't have a bridge because it's only us and the hoot owls up here, and Mrs. Stackhouse said it's a bad situation. In case any of us get sick, probably a doctor wouldn't even come. And if the house caught fire, the place would just have to burn to the ground, couldn't get any help."

"Now wasn't she a big ray of sunshine?" Mit was annoyed.

"I didn't let that bother me any," Maureen declared.

"Something else did, though, and I got to wondering. What is Miss Huckstep's name?"

Mama clattered stove lids. "You know her name. Why are you asking?"

"Because of what I saw printed in that paper. Mrs. Stackhouse got my goat, talking about her going to be an old maid. Kept going at it, she did. So I just up and told them about Miss Huckstep being secretly married."

Dad groaned. "Blatherskite! You didn't do that!"

Mama sank into a kitchen chair. "Of all people to tell. You might as well put it in the *Beaumont Banner* as to tell those two."

"I said it was a secret. Secretly married, that's what I said."

"Lotta good that will do," Mit muttered.

"Why is it so secret?" Maureen asked.

"Now you wonder why." Mama sounded disgusted. "Now you realize there might be a reason. You should think before you speak. Learn to bridle your tongue."

"Pretty hard to bridle a galloping horse," Mit chimed in.

"Maureen's tongue is tied in the middle and loose at both ends." She'd heard Dad say that before.

"Right now everybody is talking but me . . . and Walter."

"Cracker box," Walter ventured.

"But you don't tell me *why* it's a secret marriage."

Mama put wood in the stove, then opened the oven

door to check her biscuits. "She's a married woman, Maureen, secretly but legally married. Her man is a rural mail carrier, drawing regular pay. One job to a family these days, if you're lucky. Schoolboards don't hire married women."

"So you see, Miss Flap-jaw Blabbermouth, you'll cause Miss Huckstep to lose her job. She won't be hired next year." Mit pushed aside the books Maureen had brought home and sat down on the kitchen bench. "It won't matter to me. I'll be through the eighth grade and finished at Dotzero, but you're liable to have Lorene Stackhouse for a teacher."

"How do you know so much?" Maureen yelled.

"That's not hard to figure. Mit's right." Mama was always saying that. "Sterling Price Stackhouse will try his best to get elected school director and hire his niece. Dotzero district pays its taxes and gives the teacher $100 a month. Cold Spring can only pay $60."

Maureen felt miserable. She didn't know about taxes. Mit's civics class hadn't gotten to them yet.

The next morning Maureen had to go to school just as any other day. Miss Huckstep acted as if nothing had happened, and Maureen tried to do the same. But she had trouble looking directly at her. As Maureen bent over the neatest arithmetic paper she had ever prepared, she was sure Miss Huckstep's eyes were on her. Maybe she wouldn't finish the term, Maureen thought.

73

Mit might not graduate. Sooner or later Miss Huckstep would learn Maureen McCracken was the one who blabbed something that was none of her beeswax. It sure wasn't much of a way to thank a person who had taken her and Walter to visit their friends. She'd never intended to cause her teacher to lose her job.

Miss Huckstep kept all the grades busy during the morning and didn't holler but a time or two. At noon Maureen looked in the window from the playground and saw Miss Huckstep eating alone at her desk. She looked as tired as a hired girl. Miss Huckstep was just getting the hang of teaching, which wasn't easy with the Stackhouses waiting to see if she would botch the job.

Maureen realized bitterly that the Stackhouses had pumped her like a cistern. They had told her about the sawmill and people moving, about why there was no bridge. They had given her more news than the *Beaumont Banner*. But all the time they had wanted something from her. It was just the way Mama said: any dog that brings you a bone will take a bone.

After school Maureen surprised Walter. She stopped on the store porch and pushed him toward the door. "Go in and ask for mail."

"You want *me* to ask?"

"Yes, and if Mrs. Stackhouse is puffing around and pretends not to see you, speak right up. Loud."

"You ask; I'll wait."

"I'm not setting my foot in that store. I'm not going

in the U. S. post office. The Stackhouses made me so mad that I can't even talk to them."

"You must be *really* mad, Maureen."

"I am, and I'm not talking to people who are tricky to a person just trying to be friendly. Now go on before Mit gets too far ahead."

9

Mild autumn was going fast, and nobody could stop it. Darkness came now before Mit and Dad finished the evening chores. Soon there was ice in the ditch along the school road. Mit stamped right over the frozen ruts in the heavy, high-topped, laced boots he wore for school and chores.

Two of the brightest birds, the blue jays and the cardinals, stayed all winter. They hopped among the brown leaves still clinging stubbornly to the oak trees.

As Walter's cheeks reddened like coals in the cookstove, his teeth chattered, but his feet stayed warm. He appeared to have regular bird feet. Maureen hopped like the birds trying to warm hers. They were always numb when she got to school and ached as they slowly warmed in the room heated by a jacketed wood stove.

Maureen's other problem was that she wore thin cotton gloves. She'd paid no attention to the rock steps the day it snowed, and she'd been repaid with the bad luck of losing her wool gloves when her coat brushed them off the toilet seat down the hole of the school privy.

She and Walter couldn't keep up with Mit in his boots as they climbed the windy hill to school. Maureen took off her thin gloves and blew on her hands. "Mama says I have to get along with these sleazy things all winter, but I think she's knitting me some new ones for Christmas. I saw some red gloves about my size on her knitting needles, but I didn't say one thing, Walter, not one word. Making me gloves after I didn't take care of my good ones, that's what you call the spirit of Christmas. I wish I could get Mama a gift, a present to make up for her hens and for the cut-glass bowl."

"We had this story in our reader about some people so poor they couldn't buy even a tree at Christmas. That's what it said. But there are Christmas trees around everywhere." Walter pointed to a little cedar on the hill. "They're in the pasture and in the woods. Why would anybody want to pay money for one?"

"Walter Lee McCracken, everybody doesn't live in the St. Francois Mountains where cedar trees grow. People like Uncle Millard's family probably do well to have a tin Christmas tree."

"Maureen, you know those Christmas cards with pictures of houses with fireplaces and doors with wreaths on them? Do city people pay cash money for those wreaths?"

"When we get home, we'll ask Peloponnesus."

When Mama was out gathering eggs that evening, Walter and Maureen sat on the kitchen floor facing the cellar door. Maureen stared at it for quite a while before she whispered, "Every last one. That's what he says. City people have to buy every last one of those wreaths unless they have a Christmas tree growing in their yard and can hack off some limbs and make one. But most of them, if they have a tree, they baby it and don't hack anything off. That's not all. You know how Mit horsed around and broke Mama's cut-glass bowl? Peloponnesus says there's a way we can make some money and buy another bowl for Mama for Christmas."

"How?"

"Make wreaths and sell them to city people."

"We don't know any city people," Walter pointed out, "except our kinfolks and they wouldn't buy any."

"Don't worry. Peloponnesus told me how to handle that. You've got to help me make wreaths."

Walter agreed, but soon wished he hadn't as he carried armloads of prickly cedar branches, which Maureen had cut with Mama's garden pruners.

Mama let them work in the sitting room as long as they kept up the fire and cleaned the mess when they finished. The sitting room, usually cold and unused in winter, became a cozy workshop, fragrant with cedar.

Maureen took extra wire hangers from Mama's closet

and bent them into rings. Then she wired on bunches of cedar. Walter was not much good at this part of the operation, but Mit helped sometimes.

A week later Maureen admired the six finished wreaths, which were full and fat and trimmed with blue cedar berries. She felt very useful and dependable.

She explained to Walter her plan to reach city folks, and he was with her at Dotzero depot on Saturday. Walter had two wreaths; Maureen held four. Train Number 3 pulled in at 10:52 A.M. The train conductor bought a wreath from Maureen. Neither the engineer, fireman, nor brakeman wanted any.

While Pat Ash, the station agent, loaded lumpy pouches of mail into the mail car and cans of cream into the express car, Maureen and Walter walked beside the passenger coaches. Around the big, solid wheels, steam hissed out into the cold air.

Maureen held up a wreath. To her surprise, a woman motioned her aboard. She slipped up the car steps. Walter watched her walk the length of the car and come down the steps at the other end. She held her remaining wreath up to frame her smiling face.

During the next week, they made three more wreaths to replenish their stock. Saturday found them waiting again at Dotzero for Number 3. Number 6, the fast passenger train, was due first; Maureen and Walter intended to stay right on the station platform while it thundered through.

Maureen braced herself for the rush of air, but there was none. Number 6 sighed to a stop on the sidetrack. The train conductor swung down the steps of a coach, tipped his gold watch out of his pocket, and glanced at it as he hurried across the main track to Dotzero depot.

Maureen motioned Walter to follow her, and she swung up the same car steps. She spindled three wreaths on his arm, pointed to a coach door, and went in the opposite direction.

The name *Osage* shone in gold letters on the heavy door Maureen pushed open. She knew a named car was a Pullman where people rode all day, then made up their seats as beds and slept all night.

Maureen sold her wreaths right away. As she turned back down the aisle, she felt a sudden jerk, then a slight motion. She raced to the door and pulled it open. Looking down over the covered steps, she saw railroad ties jerking by in a blur. She stared out helplessly as familiar landmarks flowed by; the section house, Dotzero School, the store with Mrs. Stackhouse on the porch.

The train gathered speed. It plunged into the total darkness of Tunnel 19, and choking smoke and stinging cinders poured in. Somebody grabbed her. Daylight flashed again. It was Walter.

"Where did you come from?" a voice shouted over the roar of the train. Maureen stared at brass buttons holding a dark-blue coat closed over a fat belly. She dared look up no higher.

"We come from Dotzero," Maureen shouted. "It's no wonder you wouldn't know because Number 6 usually just tears right through Dotzero, like we didn't have a post office or anything."

"Dotzero!" the voice thundered.

"Yes, that's where we live, and it's not a nothing kind of a place either, the way some people think. My dad, he works on the railroad extra gang sometimes. He says he's extra on the extra. Well, he told us how our town got that name. When they were building the railroad, they had to plan it out so's they would know where the railroad was going. They had these surveyors that did arithmetic, and one of them put a dot and a zero down on the paper and said they had to start somewhere, so they called that place Dotzero, and that name stuck. That's where we come from, Dotzero." Maureen was hoarse from shouting.

"For crying out loud, get on out of here. This is a Pullman." Maureen got brave enough to look at the conductor's round, red face. He was eyeing Maureen's worn shoes and Walter's handed-down mackinaw. "I'm the Pullman conductor. People that ride Pullmans travel in style and comfort."

"Oh, I know that," Maureen shouted. "None of your rough travel on a Pullman. I know about the Pullman strike and everything because I listened to my brother Mit's history class. Then I listened to—"

The conductor opened the heavy door of the car and gave them a push. "Get out of here before you talk my arm off. See the regular conductor in the coach."

"Not going to see him unless he sees me first," Maureen mumbled, as she nudged Walter toward an empty seat by the window and slid in beside him. "That almost worked. I thought maybe I could keep talking until we stopped at Beaumont, and then we could get off. Oh oh, Walter, here he comes. Try to disguise yourself as an innocent, paying passenger.

Another big man in a blue coat with brass buttons stopped at their seat. "No seat check here? I must've missed you two at our Poplar Bluff stop. Tickets?" He held a big hand right under Maureen's nose.

She jabbed Walter in the ribs with her elbow. "Can't you hear the conductor? Stop looking out the window and pay attention. Give him our tickets."

Walter stared at Maureen in disbelief. "I don't have any tickets."

"You do so! I gave them to you because you have better pockets than I have."

He looked at her, mystified. "We haven't got any tickets."

"Haven't got any tickets! What would we be doing on the train if we didn't have any tickets?"

"I don't know," Walter admitted.

Maureen glanced out the window. Farms flew by. She recognized them as places near Beaumont. She turned back to the conductor and smiled. "Well, I'll have to help him look through all his pockets. He always gets the jitters when we ride on a train to our grandma's." Maureen started digging into the pockets of Walter's mackinaw. She was glad to hide her hands, which were dirty and sticky with cedar sap.

Walter had sold his wreaths too, and the conductor looked at their empty basket. "Is that all the luggage you have?"

"Yes, we always take our basket empty," Maureen explained, "because our grandma, she spoils us and gives us all kinds of stuff to bring back. Toys and everything."

Maureen started on Walter's overall pockets. The conductor stood there, tapping his big fingers on the back of the seat in front of them. He should be walking through the car, calling Beaumont station, Maureen thought. But the train continued at full speed, its whistle wailing at the crossings. They were Beaumont crossings! Flash! That was the Beaumont depot; there was the shoe factory, the feed store, the high school.

"Don't you stop at Beaumont?" Maureen asked, looking up at the conductor.

"Beaumont! This train hasn't stopped at Beaumont for two years. This is no galloping goose on a pumpkin vine, girlie. This is Number 6."

Maureen nodded. "And the company can't go stopping a big fifty-three hundred engine like this one at a place no bigger than Beaumont. Sometimes I listen to the eighth grade at our school. I heard them say it costs two dollars and thirty cents just to stop a big engine like this and start it up again. So where do you stop next?"

"St. Louis Union Station."

Maureen tried to hide her shock. It was seventy-one miles from Dotzero to Union Station. She and Walter had never been to St. Louis. Uncle Millard lived there, but she didn't know where in that big city. She pushed Walter to his feet. "Stand up, so I can search your back pockets. Mr. Conductor, I know I can find our tickets, but it'll take a while. If you come back in a little bit, maybe I'll have them."

"You better." The conductor walked slowly down the aisle.

"Stop it! Quit looking in my pockets." Walter was furious. "You know we didn't buy any tickets from Pat Ash. You're just a big fat blatherskite liar."

"Be quiet! Do you want everybody on this coach to hear you? No matter what I say, don't you dare say anything different. See all those icicles hanging off the rock out there? That's how cold it is. You want to be put off the train out in the middle of nowhere, cold as it is? Besides, this might be our only chance to see St. Louis."

"Mama will be worried," Walter said, a little calmer.

"Won't either. She's reading that new book Miss Huckstep lent her. *Gone with the Wind* is real thick. You know how she is when she gets her nose in a book. She won't know we're gone. Anyhow, we've got no choice. Now sit up straight; here he comes."

Maureen's forced laugh sounded more like a grunt. "He finally told. I like to never got it out of him. He kept taking those tickets out of his pocket, taking them out, to see if he still had them. Then he put them in his mouth so's he would know he had them, and he got to chewing on them and got them all disgusting. And he thought I'd be mad, and he swallowed half of one and thought it wouldn't be any good, so then he just threw the rest away as we got on the train."

Walter looked out the window so he wouldn't have to face the conductor.

"He looks like a pretty big boy to do a thing like that." The conductor made a hole in a little pink card with his punch and clipped it in their window shade. "I'll chance it; the run is nearly over. Do you know what a spotter is?"

"Oh, sure. If there is one on the train, and he comes and asks me, why I'll tell him the Gospel truth like I told you. I don't want to cause you to get fired for letting us stay on because we couldn't cough up the tickets. I know nowadays it's hard to get a job. Because of talking I might have caused my teacher to lose her job, only I don't know for sure. My Uncle Willard has this job in a box factory, but he might get laid off. . . ."

"Shut up; he's gone."

Maureen looked at the broad blue back going down the aisle. The conductor put his big hand on the back of each red-plush seat as he passed it.

10

Maureen sat up straight and tried to look confident. "I'm sorry I had to make you seem so dumb, Walter."

Walter sniffed. "Made me seem worse than Tisket when she was a pup, chewing up things."

The railroad right-of-way narrowed to a strip between high bluffs and the broad Mississippi River. Great jagged ice flows hung like inverted church steeples from the cliffs. On the other side of the track chunks of mud-stained ice swung in the eddies of the wide river.

First Walter pressed his face against the window, trying to see the top of the cliffs. Then he turned to stare in awe at the width of the Mississippi. Since he was only seven, going on eight, Walter hadn't thought of something that had already occurred to Maureen. If they got to the big city, how would they get home?

Bluffs and river disappeared. Except for the wail of its whistle, Number 6 ignored the towns that were getting bigger and closer together.

"I think we just went through Vicinity," Walter announced.

"Vicinity?"

"We hear it on the radio, weather for St. Louis and Vicinity."

Maureen didn't try to straighten him out. She was too fascinated by the row after row of identical houses. Maybe Uncle Millard and his family lived in one of them. There was no way to tell.

They raced by flat-roofed factories, warehouses, acres of livestock pens. Walter pointed to a building where dark smoke poured from one tall chimney and white smoke poured from another. "What's that place?"

"Factory, I guess."

"I think it's where they make the sky," Walter said.

There was a flow of railroad tracks. Then the train slowed and eased to a stop. The car darkened. They moved backward into the big, dim train shed of Union Station.

Everyone hurried off the train. Maureen and Walter hurried along with them just as if they had some place to go. They passed the Pullman car *Osage*. It seemed to Maureen about a year since she had boarded that car in Dotzero.

"Are we going to Uncle Millard's house?" Walter asked.

Maureen thought of the miles of streets and houses they had seen from the train window. If she had mailed

Mama's letter to Uncle Millard, she might have memorized the address, but Mit had been in charge. Maureen didn't see how anybody found anything in such a mess of streets. "Walter, if we spend all our time looking up kinfolks, we won't see anything of the city. We have to make the most of our chance."

It was two o'clock by the big station clock. Walter complained that he was hungry—he was getting to be a bottomless pit just like Mit—but Maureen was too excited to eat. They strolled around a little open store looking at candy bars, magazines, and all kinds of souvenirs and dit-dats.

A broad stair led to a room bigger than a barn, where the marble floors were as slick as the ice on Lost Creek. Maureen forbad Walter to skate or to act in any way as if he had never been in a big railroad station.

They ventured out into the cold streets. Strings of colored lights on lampposts and storefronts glowed in the murky, smoke-filled air. Maureen didn't know there were so many colored lights in the world. As they strolled about, she looked back frequently to make sure she could see Union Station's high, pointed tower.

The December sun disappeared behind a tall building, and Maureen's feet soon got as cold on the city sidewalks as they did on frozen country roads. As they went back to the station, Walter whined with hunger and pointed to a man selling apples near the wide, arched entrance. They spent a nickel of their wreath

89

money for one. It was a lot for just a single apple. Maureen thought of all the apples from their home orchard in their cellar and wondered how many apples were in a bushel of juicy Winesaps.

"Are we getting only one apple?" Walter asked.

"That's all for now. Let's go back out there by the train shed where we came in."

Maureen gazed up at the big board, which listed train numbers. Sure enough, there it was—Number 41, Walter's bedtime train. She felt as though she had found an old friend. They walked by the numbered gates until they came to the one for train Number 41, south to Cliff Cave, Beaumont. Dotzero wasn't listed; it didn't need to be. Anyone going to Dotzero knew Number 41 stopped there. It left in a half hour, and people were already getting on. A man in a trainman's uniform looked carefully at the ticket of each person passing through the gate.

"Give me the core of that apple, Walter. We can't buy another one. We'll have to use our money for tickets."

It wasn't as if Maureen didn't know how to stand in front of the window and buy a ticket. She'd seen Mama buy a ticket to Beaumont from Pat Ash often enough. But standing at this window was different.

"We're both half fare. How far can we get for fifty-five cents?" Maureen's voice was squeaky with nervousness.

A crabby-looking man pushed back his green eye-shade. "Oh, now, that's a new one. Which way are you going? We sell tickets to stations here. Find out where you're going."

Maureen thought of a station near St. Louis. "Cliff Cave. How much are two half fares to Cliff Cave?"

"Sixty-eight cents." The man put two tickets on the counter and held his finger ready to take the payment.

"What's the station before Cliff Cave?" Maureen asked.

"Look here, I'm selling tickets. This is not the information desk. Find out from your folks where you're going."

They found the big circular information desk, but it was very busy. The clerk looked out over their heads. Maureen watched the big clock; Number 41 would leave in seven minutes. At last, she was noticed. The station north of Cliff Cave was Coke. The information clerk took a long time to look up the half fare in a big book. It was twenty-six cents.

The ticket seller took his time too. Finally Maureen and Walter ran through the crowds, holding their tickets ready for the gateman to punch. The train conductor called all aboard as they climbed on. The brakeman tossed his little landing step up behind them and Number 41 jerked to a start.

They ducked into the first empty seat they came to on the coach.

"We don't know anybody in Coke," Walter reminded Maureen.

"I know, but we had to have tickets to get by that gateman. At first I thought I'd take the blame this time, Walter, and tell the conductor I went into the toilet and accidentally dropped the tickets down the hole the way I did my good gloves. It could happen. That's such a little bitty place in there. But anyhow, we're on and headed home."

Number 41 was a snail compared with Number 6. It eased along through what seemed to be endless city. Once it sighed to a full stop near a roofed, open pavilion. Streetlights illuminated dark forms partly wrapped in newspapers on counters under the roof.

Walter pointed. "What's that?"

"I think it's a place where they sell garden truck and the like in summer." Maureen cupped her hands around her eyes to see better from the lighted car. Suddenly she realized the dark shapes were men, lying on the counters. They had wrapped themselves in newspaper to try to shut out the cold.

"What are those things doing there? What are they?" Walter asked.

"Men with no homes, no place else to go, trying to get a night's sleep. You know, we hear about them on the radio, but I didn't know there were so many. Only a few tramps come to our door in Dotzero."

The train pulled out, and papers blowing in the

wind were all Maureen could see. As she sat back in her seat, she knew she would never forget the homeless men. She didn't know how to help them, but she did know she would always remember them, even if she lived to be older than Grandma.

When the conductor stopped at their seat a little while later, he didn't open his mouth. He just took their tickets, scribbled a number on a little card, and put it in the clip on their window shade.

The train was only a few stops out of St. Louis when the brakeman stuck his head in the car and called, "Coke, Coke station, next stop."

Maureen pulled Walter far down in the seat. "Stay down. It's like I Spy. Stay down."

Number 41 stopped briefly at Coke, then at Cliff Cave, Pevely, and Sulphur Springs. After they left Hemitite, the conductor came through the coach. He glanced at their seat check and stopped. "What's this? You kids got carried by. Why didn't you get off at Coke? Didn't you hear the station called?"

"Carried by? Now how could that be? We were sitting right here all the time, didn't go get a drink or anything," Maureen said. "But it won't matter. We can go on down the line."

"Oh, yes, it does matter, matters a heap. Your tickets are for Coke."

"Coke or some other place, about the same to us." Maureen shrugged. "By rights, we ought to have our

93

railroad pass, but I forgot it. My daddy works for the railroad."

The conductor studied them. "I seem to remember you kids from someplace, but I never saw you on my train before. What's your dad's job?"

The conductor didn't wait for an answer, however. He had to rush and see if anybody got off or on at Victoria.

"We're getting down the line, Walter," Maureen whispered. "Every stop puts us closer to Dotzero."

In no time the conductor was back at their seat, waiting for an answer to his question.

"Our dad works on the railroad extra gang, not steady, but it sure comes in handy. Last summer they painted bridges. There's a bridge right close to our house. It hasn't got any sides, just steel across to hold the ties and the track spiked to the ties. And is it ever scary walking across that thing!" Maureen paused for breath.

"Extra gang is not working for the railroad," the conductor broke in. "That's a separate contract job. So you've got no pass and no ticket either beyond Coke."

"Oh, I know it's not like regular railroading, not like Pat Ash's job. He's agent at Dotzero. I guess you know. He's the only person I know who's got just six letters in his entire name. There's a storekeeper at Dotzero named Sterling Price Stackhouse. Let's see, how many

94

letters is that?" She counted them. She told the conductor everything she could think of concerning Mr. and Mrs. Stackhouse, including the information that they were sometimes nosey. That took them as far as Beaumont.

After Beaumont, the conductor wouldn't listen anymore. He took a pad out of his pocket. "Tell me your father's name and where you live. That's all."

"Cleve McCracken. We live at Dotzero."

"That's the next stop. Get off my train."

No one else got off Number 41. Pat Ash was the only person there. His lantern and the lamp in the depot window gave some light, but even so it seemed awfully dark after the train pulled out.

Footsteps crunched on the track ballast, and a flashlight shone in Maureen's face. "Where in the name of sense have you been?" Mit demanded. "Man alive, are you going to catch it this time!" Remembering his manners, Mit turned and called, "Much obliged, Mr. Ash, for telling me you saw them here this morning."

As they trudged home Mit grumbled but held the flashlight so they could see the road. "You had everybody worried sick, and you are really going to get it."

All at once, Maureen felt so tired she could hardly put one foot in front of the other. "Did Mama finish her book?" she asked wearily.

"Yes, about suppertime. Then she realized you were

off on a wild-goose chase and had taken Walter with you. Mama says she is going to wear you out with a peach-tree switch, soon as she gets hold of you."

"Where's Dad?" Walter sounded tired too.

"Home now after calling and tramping all over our place and the Wiley place, too. He's out of heart, besides. Thinks you might have got killed on the track. I've been looking and asking all over Dotzero. Pat Ash told me he'd seen you at the depot this morning; said maybe you went on the morning train to see Grandma. You're sure going to get it for not asking."

There was no use wasting strength and breath on hardheaded Mit. Maureen decided to save both until she got home. Mit yoo-hooed before he got to the door to let Mama and Dad know they were found. By the kitchen lamp, Maureen saw that Dad looked as weary as she felt. She'd never seen his forehead wrinkles so deep. His eyes looked as if they were full of cinders.

Mama sat on the edge of a kitchen chair. Her mouth made such a straight line that her lips didn't show.

Maureen took a deep breath. "Well, we've been to St. Louis, Walter and I have. Nobody can ever say that Maureen and Walter Lee McCracken lived in the St. Francois Mountains of south Missouri and never even went anywhere or saw anything, didn't go to the city that was real close.

"We got along pretty well, considering we didn't plan it or anything. If we had, then I would have worn

96

my Sunday dress, and Walter could have worn his Sunday shirt."

Mama was still sitting on the edge of her chair. Maureen felt she might suddenly fly at her like a broody hen and flog her.

"You see, last week this woman motioned for me to get on the train when it was stopped at Dotzero and sell her one of our wreaths. She was real pretty and rich, and she had her hair rolled all around her head like a big link of baloney. I got the idea then of selling on the train. This morning Number 6 stopped on the siding at Dotzero, and we got on to sell wreaths, and the first thing I knew we were moving."

Maureen had her second wind now; her weariness was gone. She told of the coach conductor's demand for tickets. First she stood, taking the part of the gruff conductor. Then she sat and meekly squeaked her own lines. Mama relaxed enough to sit back in her chair.

"Wasn't any use spending the whole time in the depot," Maureen continued. "I wanted Walter to see something so he could tell Miss Huckstep about it. He's too bashful at school. So out we went on the street. Oh, Mama, you should have seen all the beautiful Christmas lights in the store windows, on the light posts, all the colors just everywhere.

"We went on and on down this street to a big building spread out bigger than a circus tent. In front of it there were two big bears somebody had carved out of a big rock. But they looked real soft. We touched them, didn't we, Walter, because they looked so soft? But they were stone, all right. Did you ever see them, Mama?"

"No, never did. Never saw the Christmas decorations either. Lots of things I haven't seen, but someday maybe I'll get to take a trip out West. That's where I'd like to go." There was a faraway look in Mama's eyes. Her mouth no longer looked like a line.

"I think you'll go, Mama. You never can tell what's going to happen."

Dad shook his head. "I guess you proved that today. How did you get home?"

"Here's this ticket seller. He's real sour." Maureen put on Mit's cap as a prop. She played all the parts of the scenes at the ticket window, information booth, and train gate. "It was dark when the train left St. Louis, but we saw these men wrapped up in newspapers to keep warm. Wasn't just a few either, but a lot of them. I couldn't count how many. That's where they were trying to sleep. I'll never forget those men."

Walter shivered. "I'm glad I'm home and can sleep in my bed. Was there anything left from supper?"

"That's another thing. If you travel, you ought to take a lunch, a box of fried chicken and some apples," Maureen advised.

"That was quite a show you put on for us, Maureen. Now I guess it's time for after-theater refreshment."

Mama got up and buttered slices of bread for everybody. "Kettle's hot, Cleve. I'll make you a cup of tea."

"I'd be much obliged." He didn't look so worried now.

Mama poured boiling water into the brown teapot. "You and Walter did have quite an unexpected day. So did we. I was ready to give you a good switchin', but now that I've heard your story I get the feeling you won't pull a stunt like that again."

"I won't for sure, Mama. I had hopes of earning enough money to get you another bowl, but we didn't clear a thing. Anyhow, I guess the best part about that bowl was that Uncle Millard gave it to you a long time ago. Nobody can smash that."

"Now that's about enough from you, blatherskite." Mama almost smiled. "You and Walter get up to bed."

Maureen was still awake when Mit clumped upstairs in his high boots. He stopped at her door. "You got off easy this time, but someday, Reen Peen, you're going to get into something you can't talk yourself out of."

99

11

Maureen had given Dad the idea of sending a bushel of big Wolf River apples to Uncle Millard's gang for Christmas, and the covered basket went out from the Dotzero depot by railway express with Pat Ash's assurance that it would be delivered in good condition to Uncle Millard's door, wherever that was.

Dad worried about Uncle Millard and his family. When he sat by the heating stove in the evenings, he often said he wished they lived closer so he could haul them a load of wood.

"They know they can come here," Mama reminded him. "That's what I told them in my letter. We could all warm by the same fire."

Maureen hoped Dad wouldn't get one of his black moods. If it came on near Christmas, it might last until Groundhog Day. She stopped daily at the post office to see if there was a Christmas card or any word from Uncle Millard. Though she had forgiven the Stackhouses long ago, she now guarded her talk. Any reports

100

she gave them of school included high praise for Miss Huckstep.

Clearly this year was not one to hint for Christmas presents. So Maureen didn't say one word about gifts, although she and Walter looked at the toy section of the Sears Roebuck catalog until the pages came loose.

At Walter's request, Maureen read aloud the description of his favorite cowboy suit: heavy duck trousers with imitation leather, metal rivet trim, fringed yoke, cotton twill shirt, red banana handkerchief.

"That's bandanna handkerchief," Mit corrected. "Now pipe down. Walter can read that to himself. I've got to learn all these parts by heart for the Christmas program."

Maureen had already memorized her recitation. Miss Huckstep had picked a very long one for her, so it must be that she still didn't know Maureen had blabbed to the Stackhouses. Otherwise, she would have given her just a short baby piece. Or maybe Miss Huckstep knew and had forgiven her for being such a blatherskite.

Even so Maureen wished she had as many parts in the Christmas program as Mit, who got to be the father in every dialogue. There were not many big kids left at school since the sawmill had closed and two more families had moved away.

Mit had all his parts down pat when the time came for their afternoon program, which would close Dotzero School for Christmas vacation. Maureen knew her recitation so well that she had to put on the brakes to keep from saying it too fast. At the end of the program, Miss Huckstep handed out an extra-good treat of a bag of candy and an orange for each pupil.

That night sleet rattled the dormer window by Maureen's bed. When Dad came in the next morning with a pail of Molly's milk, he pronounced the day a real bone snapper.

Mama wanted to go with them to cut the Christmas tree, but she was afraid she'd fall and break a hip. Nothing could have kept Maureen indoors, though. She and Walter slid and fell keeping up with Mit, who cracked the ice with his heavy boots as they searched for the best Christmas tree.

They were deep in the woods when the sun broke through gray clouds. Sunlight on the ice-covered trees was more beautiful than all the colored lights Maureen and Walter had seen in St. Louis.

Mit was so particular. Maureen's feet and fingers were aching with cold by the time he agreed that a full, well-shaped cedar, greener than most, would do. They slid and dragged it home and set it up in the sitting room. As the room warmed from the heating-stove fire Mit had built, the cedar gave off the exciting fragrance that always meant Christmas to Maureen.

By Christmas Eve the tree was trimmed with foil-covered stars, strings of popcorn, and fifteen yards of paper chains made by Maureen and Walter. As she looked at the decorated tree, Maureen wished that Rose could see it.

Christmas morning Mama covered the oilcloth on the kitchen table with their Turkey red cloth, and Maureen put a bowl of cedar twigs and blue berries in the center of the table. Then she and Walter went in the wagon with Dad to meet Grandma, who was coming to Dotzero on Number 3.

They could smell the roast chicken before they opened the kitchen door. There was sage in the dressing, whipped cream on the baked apples, and vanilla sauce on the suet pudding. For a while after dinner Maureen had a very tight feeling around her middle. She didn't want to move.

"I haven't eaten that much for a month of Sundays." Grandma folded her napkin. "It makes me feel guilty, though, when I think about Millard and Cora and all those little ones. Wonder what kind of day they're having. They're always on my mind. In my last letter, I sent them a postal money order for Christmas. It won't help much, but I can't write checks now since my bank failed. Sometimes I feel like my courage has failed too." Grandma fell silent.

Maureen looked at Dad. His smile had faded and a worried look had come into his eyes. It was time to cheer everyone up. Maureen recalled the Christmas program and recited her piece at both slow and fast speeds. She also recited a longer piece she had made

103

up, which she thought was better. Since she had memorized all the dialogue, she took all the parts and did two complete dramas.

At that point Mama mentioned the sunshine outside and told her and Walter to go out for some fresh air.

Walter climbed into the tire swing. "The tree in the house is just a cedar tree with paper stuff hung on it. Why does it feel like a different day, not a regular Wednesday?" he asked.

"Because it's Christmas, and it's Christmas because you feel different, and don't you forget it, Walter."

"Do you think Santa Claus couldn't get across Lost Creek?"

"Now just watch out what you're saying, Walter Lee McCracken. Santa Claus doesn't keep track of everything, writing it all down like a store bill—who wants what and how much and all. Christmas puts trimming on winter, just the way we put trim on that tree. Remember, there may be lots of kids running around in new cowboy suits today, but they don't have real live mules like our Fox and Jack. They don't have a cow like Molly either. Her cream is so thick you can hardly pour it out of a pitcher."

A hen cackled in the chicken house. "That hen just laid an egg," Walter observed. "Uncle Millard doesn't have any chickens."

"Well, of course not. They haven't got a cellar full of apples either. That's what worries Grandma. We'd need a big house for Uncle Millard's family." Maureen jerked the tire swing to a stop. "We can make our playhouse bigger. Do you remember the one we built last summer, over there by the gate? It's not too cold to work outside. We'll make it big enough for us and our cousins, too, in case they come."

They brushed dirt and dried grass off the rows of rocks that marked the rooms of their summer playhouse. Carrying more rocks from the hillside into the yard was hard work. Then came the easy part of placing them side by side to outline the floor plan of added rooms. Anything aboveground was left to the imagination.

When it was time for Grandma to leave to catch the train back to Beaumont, Mama and Dad came outside with her. As they waited for Mit to bring the wagon around, Mama looked at the playhouse. "My goodness! Have you kids been packing more rocks into the yard?"

"Not just rocks," Maureen explained. "We're building more rooms on the playhouse, in case Uncle Millard's family come. You see, here's the kitchen—"

"I'll see later, Maureen. Come now and tell your grandma good-bye."

Grandma kissed everybody and cried and said she thought it was her last Christmas. She missed Millard and his family and thought something terrible was amiss because they had sent her a cheerful card but hadn't come to see her.

It was enough to put Dad into a black mood, but instead his gray eyes twinkled. "Don't worry, Grandma. We'll build a couple of rooms on the house the way Maureen and Walter have enlarged their playhouse. Millard's family can move here to Dotzero, and we can all celebrate Christmas together next year."

12

It hadn't come out even like a long-division problem that was correct, but still Maureen felt she had made up somewhat for the broken bowl and the slain hens. She considered her demonstration of building on to a house her Christmas present to her entire family, including Uncle Millard.

Dad was really serious about adding two rooms to the McCracken house. The day after Christmas he bargained with the extra-gang boss for scrap lumber left from a job, and he got it dirt cheap. Although they didn't tell Grandma, not wanting to get her hopes too high, Dad and Mit began hauling the lumber while the good weather held. When the McCracken hogs were sold, there should be enough cash for the needed windows, doors, hardware, and roofing.

Maureen and Walter continued to equip their playhouse. They searched the Wiley place for salvageable junk. That's where they were when they learned Grandma was sick.

Maureen was breathless from running when she told Mama. "Walter and I chased right home to tell you about Grandma. We were over by the Wiley house, and *chug-chug* up the lane comes Mrs. Wiley in her Durant. Walter wanted to hide, and I wouldn't let him. Makes it look like we were meddling around there, which we weren't. You know if you act as if you've done—"

"About your grandma, Maureen?"

"Well, I was just as polite as you please, said howdy and all. Then I shut up tight as her pocketbook and listened to her. And do you know what she is thinking about doing? She told me, out and out. She's thinking about tearing down the Wiley house. She said she didn't want tramps and such using it, making fires, maybe setting her woods afire. And she said her husband that's up in the cemetery would rather know it was torn down than that it fell down, and besides, if there was no house, the taxes would be lower."

"You haven't got to the part about your grandma."

"She didn't either for a long time, did she, Walter? All at once, she looked at us as if she just figured out who we were. She stared at me with her bug eyes as if I didn't know *b* from a bull's foot, didn't know how to pound sand in a rathole—"

"Maureen!" Mama was getting impatient.

"—and she says, 'Now you tell your mama this.' And she turns to Walter and says, 'If your sister doesn't get it straight, you tell your mama—' "

"Tell me what?" Mama demanded.

"That Grandma has come down with the flu so bad it might go into pneumonia."

"Bad news and more of it. Your grandma would never pull through pneumonia, frail as she is." Mama bit her lip. "I'll just have to get ready to go to Beaumont and stay with her until she is better."

"Can we go too?" Walter asked.

"You might catch the flu. Then I'd have three down with it. You're better off here at home, where Maureen will be needed anyhow."

"For what, Mama?"

"Oh, for lots of things." Mama looked at the kitchen clock. "Now let me think. Maybe I'll have time to catch Number 32 if I get a move on. It's a good thing I've finished the ironing and have clean things to pack." She gathered up a stack of clothes from her worktable and left the room.

Maureen picked up the slip and blouse Mama had dropped and followed her into the hall. "Do you have to go away now? It's still Christmas."

"Sickness doesn't pick a time. You'll have plenty to do." Mama opened the door to the cold sitting room. "You can take down the Christmas tree for starters. It's dry enough to set the house afire."

Maureen and Walter shook with cold as they unwound paper chains from the tree. "Nope, it's *not* still Christmas," Maureen said. "It's over, and this is an awful job. It's like working to pay for a dead horse."

By the time Mama was ready to leave, the Christmas tree lay in the yard, bits of tinsel blowing from its twigs. When Dad and Mit finally showed up with the wagon, they took Mama and her suitcase to Dotzero. Maureen looked after them sadly.

The first few days Mama was gone, Maureen and Walter kept each other company. Dad and Mit were usually away, either hauling lumber or hunting. All during small-game season, Mit was allowed to use the twenty-gauge shotgun.

The extra Christmas food didn't last long. Mit was always hungry. Two days after Mama left, Maureen watched him and Dad put on their heavy mackinaws, ready to go out into the morning cold.

"Will you be home for dinner?" she asked.

"Yes, about noon. It takes a half day for Fox and Jack to make the trip for lumber. You're chief cook," Dad said, hurrying out the door.

"What shall I cook, Dad?" Maureen called after him.

"How about rabbit? There's half a dozen, skinned and dressed, hung up on the back porch."

Maureen and Walter watched the wagon go down the hill toward Lost Creek. The house was lonesome without Mama, so they stayed outside and got chilled to the bone playing in the tire swing. After they waved at Number 3 going by, Maureen knew the time had come to stir up the fire and fix dinner.

The rabbit carcasses hung in a stiff row from the porch rafter. The dark-red flesh was covered with a bluish membrane. They were frozen hard.

Walter looked up at the skinned rabbits. "I'm glad they didn't hunt for anymore today. We've got enough."

"Yes, and because I'm a girl instead of a boy like you, I'm supposed to know how to cook a froze rabbit."

Maureen sulked for a moment and then determinedly brought a chair from the kitchen, climbed up on it, cut down the biggest rabbit, and took it inside. Even with Mama's sharpest knife, she had trouble severing the joints. But she knew it had to be cut in pieces, or she could never get it in the skillet. She hacked and pulled on the icy meat until she had six pieces—four legs and the body cut in two. Her hands were freezing.

She poked kindling into the coals in the cook stove. Over the crackling fire, the lard in the skillet melted to hot, clear liquid. Maureen stood back and tossed the cold meat into the skillet. The hot fat spattered, and she jumped in pain as it hit her hands.

After a bit she got closer and with a big cooking fork turned a piece over in the skillet. Sure enough, it was brown on one side. Maybe it wouldn't be so hard to cook rabbit after all.

When Mit and Dad returned at noon, stamping their

feet from the cold, the pieces were nicely browned on both sides. Maureen felt proud as she placed them on a platter. Besides rabbit, there were some of Dad's drop biscuits left over from breakfast, a crock of skim milk, and a quart of canned blackberries.

Mit took the biggest piece from the platter and eagerly bit into the meat. A shocked look came over his face. He spit out black pellets and held his jaw. "It's full of shot! I almost broke a tooth."

Dad spit out his bite. "You should have dug out the shot with a sharp knife, Maureen. And you didn't get this near done. It's downright raw and cold next to the bone."

Maureen turned a piece on the platter. "It's brown all over, like cooked meat."

"It's awful," Mit howled. "I'm hungry, and it's raw and full of shot."

"It takes a while to tenderize game. I guess you didn't cook it long enough," Dad explained.

"If I had cooked it anymore, it would have burned," Maureen argued.

Mit got up from the table. "Reen Peen can't do anything right. She can't do any work at all, just blab, blab. That's all you can get out of old Reen Peen."

"You should have told me yesterday," Maureen defended herself. "Then I could have brought the rabbit inside and let it thaw out."

112

Mit snorted. "Lotta good that would have done."

"Would so too, because I tell you froze rabbit is something hard to handle. Walter and I feel bad anyhow to think about how this bunny used to be hopping around, soft and all."

"You eat plenty when Mama's here to cook it."

Maureen took a deep breath. "Well, but then—"

"Stop chewing the rag, both of you. I should have known that cooking rabbit right would be too hard for Maureen." Dad finished his biscuits and blackberries, got up from the table, and turned on the radio. "I want to hear this livestock report. I've been holding off selling our hogs in hopes the price would go up to something more reasonable. Then if Sterling Stackhouse can get his truck across the creek, I'll have him haul those porkers to market."

Dad wanted absolute quiet when he listened to the noon livestock market report broadcast from National Stockyards, Illinois. Mit, not able to complain aloud, made sickening faces and held his stomach as if he were starving.

"When rabbit is all cooked up with onions and brown gravy, it's different," Maureen whispered. "But for all I know that rabbit I cooked was the one Tisket chased every evening last summer in the orchard. It was a regular pet."

"Baloney bulls are steady," the radio announced.

113

"And when that rabbit ran by, I'd say to it, 'Rabbit, Rabbit, you're looking mighty thin.' " In a louder voice, Maureen spoke for the rabbit. " 'Yes, sir, yes, sir, but I'm cuttin' through the wind.' "

"Turning now to the hog market . . ." the radio reported.

"Simmer down. I want to hear this." Dad moved closer to the radio.

Maureen put her words to a tune, singing out, " 'Mr. Rabbit, Mr. Rabbit, your coat's mighty gray.' " She no longer felt bad about the dreadful dinner.

"Light hogs of medium quality, three cents a pound, a record low," the radio crackled.

" 'Oh, yes, sir, it's made that way.' " Maureen sang and jumped like a scared rabbit.

"Great heavens above!" Dad yelled. He swung his big hand. Its full force landed on the side of Maureen's head. "Can't you be still? You drive a person to distraction!" Cold air fanned into the kitchen as Dad went out and slammed the door.

Maureen was stunned from the blow and from the fact that Dad had hit her. Even Mit looked a little shocked. Without a word, he followed Dad.

Maureen held back tears as long as she could. Then she huddled on the floor in front of Peloponnesus and cried. Without looking up, she reached for a towel from the kitchen rack. As she wiped her eyes she felt the roughness of its lace trim. She had grabbed her San-

114

soucie keepsake towel, which was displayed on the rack for show. Maureen stared at the pattern of coarse pink lace and thought of her friends at Cold Spring.

She replaced the towel on the rack and saw Walter sitting on the linoleum in a warm patch of sunlight, which shone from the south window. On such an afternoon, the Sansoucies would be out playing for sure.

"Can you hear all right?" Walter asked.

"Yeah, I can hear, but he should not have hit me like that when Mama is gone and it's lonesome." Maureen stared at Peloponnesus. After much nodding, she turned again to Walter. "Peloponnesus says we can't do anything about the hog market, but we can do something for ourselves. He says there is no use staying here the rest of the day in this kitchen full of dirty dishes. Walter, without asking, we're going to hightail it over to the Sansoucies."

"Not me!"

"I'd catch it worse if I let you stay by yourself. I'll tell Dad I made you go with me, which is Gospel truth. I am."

The old wagon road, not good enough for cars, was the shortest way over the two hills and through the one hollow to the Sansoucies. Maureen walked fast. Walter and Tisket trotted along behind her. They passed the Cold Spring School, which had faded paper Santas pasted in the windows.

It seemed that in no time they could hear the Sansoucies playing in the distance. That sound was better than music to Maureen. A big game of Prison Base came to a halt so that both sides could give them a welcome, which made Maureen feel very important.

Rose grasped Maureen's hands. "I knew you'd come again the way you promised."

"No school, so we thought we might as well visit. Only we can't stay very long because it gets dark so early now. And we're walking this time," Maureen said.

While new sides were being chosen, Maureen told Rose they had walked by the school. "Did you make one of the Santas in the window?" she asked.

Rose marked the thawed ground with the toe of her worn shoe. "We haven't gone yet."

"You better start, Rose, right after vacation. If you don't, you might not get promoted."

"I know, and then I'd be too big for my class and not want to go to school anymore. I want to go now, but Lorene Stackhouse is the teacher, and my folks think she might have it in for us. Then, too, we don't have decent clothes."

When the children went into the house later to warm themselves by the heating stove, Maureen had the entire Sansoucie family as an audience for her description of her trip to St. Louis. They listened as if she were the "March of Time" radio broadcast.

At the end of the story, Mrs. Sansoucie took up her

crocheting. "I don't see how you could take the risk of getting on that big train. I'd be scared of a train wreck."

"How about the conductor? He gets on it everyday, just about every day of his life," Maureen pointed out. "But he's not so brave. He might be afraid to live out here on this farm the way you do."

"How did you know what to do in that big depot with all them trains?" Mr. Sansoucie wanted to know. "I wouldn't know what to do in a place like that."

"Oh, I read the list of Missouri Pacific trains and found Number 41. Then I read the signs on the gates. And, of course, I could read all the other signs in the station and out on the street, too. I could have read the thick book that gave the ticket costs, but they wouldn't let me see it. It's mighty handy to be able to read."

"Yes, I guess it is," Mrs. Sansoucie agreed. Maureen watched her pull one loop of thread through another. That's all there was to crocheting, but she was making a pretty pattern.

Walter nudged Maureen and pointed to the west window.

Maureen nodded. "We've got to get home. It'll soon be sundown."

Mr. Sansoucie studied the evening sky for a few minutes. "Yes, and a cold night coming. I'm proud you came to see us. I wish we still lived neighbors. We've had to move so much that our kids are getting behind in their books, but they're starting at Cold Spring next week. You can tell Alma Huckstep that."

When Maureen and Walter started home, Rose went with them as far as Cold Spring School, carrying one of her little sisters. She looked at the one-room white building and then smiled shyly at Maureen. "I'd be braver starting here if I had you to talk for us, Maureen." Her smile widened. "But we're coming, even if our clothes don't look like a Sears order. We're coming. You heard my dad say so."

Rose stood on the road waving until she was little more than a speck on the horizon. After they had turned around for the last time, Maureen and Walter ran down the first hill. As they started up another, Maureen stopped and felt her eyetooth.

"Does your jaw still hurt?" Walter asked.

"No, but I think I might have got a tooth knocked loose."

"Dad didn't have hardly any dinner," Walter reminded her.

"You think I don't know anything? And he heard that hog market report, too, even if it wasn't still enough to hear a pin drop. He was counting on cash from our hogs to get stuff we need to finish the rooms. Now there won't be enough. So I got this awful slap."

"We ran away, and he'll be extra hungry for supper." Walter's eyes were as sad and serious as a hound's.

"He can't be as mad as he was, Walter. I'm not as mad at him either."

When they came to the brow of the last hill, Walter pointed down to Fox and Jack, standing in the barn lot. "They're back before us."

Maureen listened at the back door. "I hear Dad whistling," she whispered. Then she flung open the door. "We're back, and I think we did some good, too. Miss Huckstep thinks it's a downright shame that the Sansoucies don't go to school. So we went over there because I didn't want to be miserable a whole afternoon of Christmas vacation, and that's what I was, Mama gone and all, so we went to visit the Sansoucies. Maybe I talked them into going to school. Their dad said they would go."

Maureen watched Dad stir batter in a crock. "What are you making? Want me to do that? I'll do whatever you say."

"I'm making us some flapjacks for supper. A couple of eggs would make them rise right off the griddle. Run out to the hen house and gather the eggs before they freeze. Then we'll have to get all these dishes washed after supper. I saw Mrs. Wiley on the road. She tells me Grandma is much better. Mama's coming home tomorrow morning."

"Oh, I'm glad to hear that."

"So am I," Walter agreed.

119

"I was glad to hear it myself," Dad said. "Kind of saved the day. Sitting in the wagon, watching the mules' ears flop, I had time to think. We'll manage somehow, cash or no cash. We've always managed."

Maureen picked up the round-bottomed egg basket and motioned Walter to follow her. Outside she swung the empty basket over her head. Although Dad had not said so, Maureen thought he was sorry he had slammed her on the side of the head. He had kept himself out of a black mood even though his only girl blabbed during the livestock report and couldn't cook rabbit.

"Walter, I wanted you to come along because we might find an angel's egg. Sometimes about sunset, if there's a pink one like tonight, you might find one right in a hen's nest. Look for one. It'll be real big."

13

That very night Walter woke everyone up crying because of a terrible pain in his stomach. Mit said that came from eating raw rabbit and being dragged up hill and down dale by Maureen. Dad was ready to go to the Stackhouses' store and call Dr. Varney in Beaumont. Then, just at daybreak, Walter fell asleep. He was still sleeping peacefully when Mama came home from Grandma's. Maureen imitated Walter's cries, but she was not sure she had convinced Mama of how sick Walter had been.

He got better, but he didn't stay better. Every week or so he would get a gut pain that just about bent him double. Then it would go away, and Walter soon would be out running on hard, frozen ground and skating on the ice of Lost Creek.

One day the wind blew warm instead of chill, and rain fell. Everything was soft and wet. The road to Dotzero was muddy as a hog wallow. Ice broke loose, and water rose in Lost Creek. Mit, Maureen, and Wal-

121

ter just made it across their footbridge after school. The February thaw had come.

Walter's cries woke the family again that night. Mama felt his forehead and said that he was burning up with fever. The pain had never been so bad.

The kitchen clock struck five when Dad decided to start for the store to call Dr. Varney. As Maureen and Mama followed him downstairs to the kitchen, Maureen remembered that Mrs. Stackhouse had said it would be hard for them to get a doctor. "Will Dr. Varney come?" she asked anxiously.

"He'll come if I can get hold of him. He knows he'll get paid sooner or later. McCrackens are good pay," Dad said. "He won't have a twenty-mile round trip for nothing."

Mama walked the floor. "It rained all night, and it's still raining. The Dotzero road is a loblolly of mud. Even if he slid over the road, Dr. Varney couldn't cross Lost Creek in that new, low car of his."

Dad lighted the barn lantern. "Fox and Jack can ford it. After I telephone, I'll wait at Dotzero and bring Dr. Varney here in the wagon. We'll get him here to see Walter."

Mama looked out the kitchen window. "It's still pitch dark, Cleve. I dread for you to go into the ford."

"It'll soon be dawn, Lillian, and I know the current. You get back upstairs to Walter."

Mama sponged Walter's face and chest with cold

water to try to bring the fever down. Then Walter asked Mit to play the French harp to make the waiting easier.

Maureen felt useless. She had to do something, so she went downstairs and put on her coat, then found her rubbers and Mama's umbrella. Tisket followed her to the creek ford where the footbridge was underwater. They waited in the rain for the wagon to return.

Tisket heard it first and barked. When the flopping ears of the mules came in view, Maureen thought they were a beautiful sight. Through them she could see two big, dark figures hunched against the rain on the wagon seat. Dad watched the water surging around the wheels as Fox and Jack forded the creek. He didn't notice Maureen. By the time she ran up her shortcut path, Dr. Varney was already in the house. In his big, dripping slicker, he seemed to fill the whole kitchen. Maureen thought that being someone like Dr. Varney whom folks were always glad to see must be wonderful. She wished she could be a person like him.

Dr. Varney pushed different places on Walter's stomach. When he pressed one spot, Walter yelled with pain.

Dr. Varney sat down beside the bed. "You say he's had these attacks before? How many?"

"First one was right after Christmas." Maureen started to count on her fingers. "And then. . . ."

Mama touched her shoulder. "Be quiet, Maureen."

"But I remember. The next one was on the way home from school. . . ."

"Shut up," Mit hissed.

"I'd say about five, Doctor, but this is the worst," Mama said. "He's been in pain since about midnight."

Dr. Varney led the way into the hallway. "I believe he has appendicitis. We've got to get him to the hospital at once. If surgery is postponed, the appendix will rupture. That is very dangerous."

Dad's face looked bleak and strained. "You saw that creek ford. The ambulance couldn't get here. We'll have to take him out by wagon as far as Dotzero."

Dr. Varney shook his head. "Slick, rutty road in a slow wagon is not good. Any jarring is dangerous. You folks are so cut off here without a bridge. We've got to get that boy to St. Louis and into a hospital." He spoke very quietly.

"I know something we could do," Maureen announced.

"Pipe down," Mit whispered. "Dangerous! You heard what the doctor said. Do you want Walter to know how sick he is?"

"Number 6, that fast train Walter and I rode to St. Louis, will go right by our house." No one seemed to hear Maureen or notice when she slipped downstairs. As she put on her soggy coat, she spoke to the cellar door. "Peloponnesus, you know how bad Walter is, and you know I've got to help him, so wish me luck."

124

At the railroad bridge, Maureen checked the block signal to be sure no train was coming. She'd never crossed the trestle alone. Now she had to get over it by herself in the pouring rain.

She gritted her teeth and stepped onto the bridge. Tisket whined and followed. "Go back, Tisket. I'll do well to take care of myself."

She was over in no time. It was only a mile and a half to Dotzero, and she was a fast runner. As she ran, she repeated: *declarative, imperative, exclamatory, interrogative.* She ran until her side hurt and her throat was dry.

Maureen could see Pat Ash in the depot bay window, which faced the track. She ran right through the waiting room into the agent's office. "Mr. Ash," she panted. "You have to stop Number 6 at the trestle by our house. Walter has appendicitis. Dr. Varney says we have to get him to the hospital in St. Louis. Stop the train, and we'll put Walter in the express car the way you do a veal calf. It's the fastest way to get him there."

"Hold on, Maureen. I can't just up and stop a fast train. Do you think I'm president of the railroad, some bigwig or official? I'm just the agent here at Dotzero."

"You can *try*, Mr. Ash," Maureen pleaded. "We're good pay for shipping Walter. If you don't even try, you'll be sorry you didn't. Number 6 won't jolt him like a mule wagon would."

Telegraph instruments rattled on Pat Ash's table.

125

There was a telephone by his desk, too, but it wasn't like the one at the store. The agent drew it out on its adjustable rack. Curved wires over his head held the receiver to his ear, leaving his hands free to write down the train dispatcher's orders.

"Dispatcher. Dotzero. I've got a girl here, wants Number 6 stopped at Milepost 72, Bridge 43. Yes, that's what I told her. Oh, I'd say about ten or eleven years old."

Pat Ash flinched and covered the mouthpiece with his hand. "He's cussin' a blue streak. I knew he would. Says he doesn't know what I'm talking about."

"I'll tell him." Maureen took the receiver off Pat Ash's head and put it on her own damp hair. She'd never talked on any kind of telephone before, let alone one with a mad train dispatcher on the other end. "Mr. Dispatcher, this is Maureen McCracken. My brother Walter, he's eight now, has got this appendicitis about to bust. Lost Creek is way up so the ambulance can't get across to our house, and the wagon is too rough on the mud road. We might not get Walter out in time. But if you stop Number 6, Walter could go right to St. Louis and to the hospital. We'd get him on real fast so it wouldn't mess up your railroading."

There was some awful cussing, then Maureen heard very clearly, "Where's Ash?"

Maureen handed him the receiver. He wrote, re-

126

peated, and spelled out the numbers of a train order. "Train number 6, s-i-x, stop Bridge 43, f-o-u-r t-h-r-e-e, Milepost 72, s-e-v-e-n t-w-o, pick up express, emergency patient for St. Louis isolated by high water, depart 11:09, e-l-e-v-e-n n-i-n-e."

Pat Ash looked at his pocket watch. "Here's a copy of the train order the dispatcher's giving Number 6 at Arcadia. You've got very little time to run back and tell your folks to have Walter on the right-of-way. Make sure you check the block signal at the trestle."

Maureen ran back faster than she'd come. She had to get across the trestle before Number 6 came into the block. She was almost at the bridge when she saw the wagon coming slowly down the rainswept hill. She yelled and waved her arms. They saw her; Mama waved back. Maureen called out her message, but she knew she couldn't be heard for the roar of Lost Creek.

Mit hopped off the wagon and was soon scrambling up the railroad embankment. He came toward her across the trestle. "What are you trying to do, Maureen, yelling like that? You want to scare Fox and Jack into a runaway? Get over this bridge before Number 6 comes into the block."

Maureen panted for breath and pointed to the milepost on the opposite side of the bridge. "It's going to stop for Walter, over there." She handed Mit the crumpled copy of the train order.

He read it, then without another word to her he turned back and bounded across the trestle ties, two at a time.

Maureen tried to follow him, but suddenly the thought of being high over swirling water made her so dizzy that she couldn't set foot on the bridge.

Number 6 came into the block. From the safety of the right-of-way, Maureen saw that Mit had reached the wagon. She watched Dad and Dr. Varney hold the ends of a blanket so that it formed a stretcher and carry Walter up to the track as carefully as if he were a setting of angel's eggs.

Number 6 whistled for a crossing. It seemed to be coming as fast as ever. No, there was a difference. It was easing to a full stop. Hands reached out of the express car to take hold of Walter's blanket. Dad climbed up into the car. Maureen had a glimpse of the top of Walter's head; then the train, Walter, and Dad were gone.

Mit drove the mules across the ford and stopped at the foot of the embankment below Maureen. She wished he would come up and carry her down piggyback, but she knew that was out of the question.

Somehow she got down the bank, and Mama helped her into the wagon. "Maureen! How did you do that? A big, fast train! Did you get Pat Ash to stop it?"

"I guess so, but now I feel powerful weak."

"Well, no wonder!"

"When I had to cross the bridge to help Walter, I didn't have trouble, but just now I couldn't get back across it to save me."

Mama hugged Maureen, wet as she was. "It's like the sermon text on Sunday. 'Perfect love drives out fear.' "

Maureen began to cry. "I do love Walter, even when I tell him things I make up. I didn't even get to tell him good-bye."

"You did a very remarkable thing for your brother, Miss Maureen," Dr. Varney said. "Don't worry now. You folks get me back to my car at Dotzero. I'll call the hospital from the store and have an ambulance meet the train. All of you get in the dry. I don't want to be called back across Lost Creek to treat pneumonia."

"We'll get across before the water gets higher," Mama said, excited with relief. "This is a young team and fractious at times, but we'll make it."

14

Walter's operation was just in time. If Maureen hadn't stopped the fast train, he never would have made it. Everyone agreed on that, so Maureen didn't have to say so herself. Whenever she was praised, she warmed with pride and satisfaction.

As jam-packed as it was, Dad had stayed at Uncle Millard's until Walter was ready to come home from the hospital. Besides losing his plump apple cheeks and getting a scar on his stomach, Walter was just the same. He wasn't a bit stuck up because he'd had an operation.

At school Mit didn't grumble about the number of times Maureen told of stopping Number 6. Miss Huckstep let her repeat the story frequently, as long as she said blankety-blank-blank for the train dispatcher's swearing. Walter was her best audience. His cheeks were thinner, but he still smiled his eyes shut when Maureen described her run in the rain. She included great leaps to show him how she crossed the trestle.

They had Walter home, and now Dad wanted to bring Uncle Millard's family to the farm, too. He had seen with his own eyes how bone-hard things were for them. The box factory had shut down. Aunt Cora got a day's work now and then trimming hats in a factory.

Maureen made herself keep still as Mama and Dad talked of Uncle Millard's family. "We could get by now, especially with summer coming. Some of the kids could sleep on the floor," Mama said.

Dad nodded. "So I told him, but he won't bring his gang, bag and baggage, and pile in on top of us. You know Millard is stubborn as a Missouri mule, stubborn as Fox and Jack put together. He's proud, too. Years back he left the farm and Dotzero and said no more cornbread living for him. He'd be ashamed as a whipped dog to come back empty-handed now."

"When we're ready to frame up the rooms, he could help," Mama suggested.

"It'll be many a day before we get to that. Hospital bill will take the cash, farming and extra-gang work will take the time." A gloomy look came over Dad's face.

"Cleve, it's spring, Walter was spared to us. I'm going to put in extra garden. I believe Millard's gang will be here to eat it by the middle of the summer."

Maureen liked to imagine their yard and hillside noisy with many cousins, playing games she directed.

131

The Sansoucies could come and stay all day. Summer would soon arrive; there were already lots of signs of spring.

A patch of waxy, white flowers bloomed at the edge of the cindery railroad embankment. On the way home from school the next day, Maureen stopped to pick some.

"You'd better get on home and help Mama," Mit ordered.

"I'm just getting a couple of bloodroot flowers to give Walter some freckles." Reddish fluid oozed from the flower stems, and Maureen dotted some on Walter's nose. "He still looks kind of peaked."

"Someday Walter won't stand still for you, Maureen." Mit was forever predicting a day when a lot of awful things would happen. Maureen thought he was grouchy because he hadn't been able to miss a single day of school to help Dad plant potatoes. He had to study for his eighth-grade examination. Then he'd be through. Someday she would miss Mit at school, but Maureen wasn't going to tell him and make him a worse swellhead than ever.

Right now she was glad it was spring. Creek willows were leafing out the color of lettuce. Beside the short-cut path, a little shad tree had burst into bloom, like popcorn in a hot skillet. With white patches flashing, a mockingbird flew up to the peak of the dormer window and began imitating all the birds of the St. Francois Mountains.

"Now, Walter, you take that mockingbird. Suppose you never heard one and I told you there was a bird with a little bitty brain and that it could sing like any other bird, even *meow* like a cat. You'd say it was a big fib, couldn't be. But you hear it, so you know it's true."

Walter, tuckered out, just nodded and trudged on.

When they reached home, Maureen wandered off alone across the pasture toward the Wiley house. Spring beauties, bluets, and Johnny-jump-ups misted the short spring grass. She remembered the wild pansies and raced over the flowery carpet to the clay bank where they had bloomed the year before. There they were, blooming away. Maureen picked some of the flowers, which looked like extra-large lavender violets. She especially liked the ones with two velvety, dark-purple upper petals.

At home she showed them to Mama. "Look at these. It's just the way you said. These wild pansies are right where they were last year, same as ever."

"Spring and the sun haven't failed us yet." Mama pointed to tomato seedlings growing in an old dishpan on her worktable. They were all slanting toward the south window. "I sure liked working outside all day. I got the ground ready to put in extra garden for Millard and the family."

"When school is out, I'll help," Maureen promised. "Garden dirt isn't like house dirt, is it?"

"Not one bit." Mama was sure of that.

At school Miss Huckstep made them work even though they were on the last chapters of their textbooks. She didn't act like a teacher who wasn't returning. Maybe she still didn't know that Maureen had spilled the beans to the Stackhouses. If her big mouth had caused Miss Huckstep to lose her job, Maureen didn't know how she would ever make it up to her.

There was always a basket dinner on the last day of school. Usually there was a program given by the graduating eighth grade, too. But this year only a dinner was planned for the closing day in April. Two more families had moved away, which left Mit the only one finishing eighth grade. Miss Huckstep just handed him his diploma and made jokes about his being the best in his class.

It was warm enough to eat outdoors, so long boards were set on carpenter's horses to make a table. Miss Huckstep helped Mama set out baked beans, potato salad, and the cured ham she'd brought. "Alma, I want you to know we think you did a first-class job your first year of teaching, and, regardless of anything, we hope you get your school back." Mama lowered her voice. "I see Sterling P. Stackhouse, our new school director, is taking an interest. He's right here ready to tie into the eats. What does he say about next term?"

"I can't tell what's going on." Maureen could hardly hear Miss Huckstep. "I wrote out my application and gave it to him a month ago. Every day I go into the store to give him an opportunity to tell me if I'm hired for next year. He just hems and haws something about a confused situation. So it leaves me uncertain. Sometimes I think he's waiting to see if his niece, Lorene, gets her school back at Cold Spring. If not, he'll get her in here."

Miss Huckstep unwrapped a stack of paper plates. "Of course, he may have another reason not to hire me. Yesterday I got a letter at the post office addressed to Miss Alma Huckstep. Mrs. Stackhouse held on to it as if it belonged to her and asked me twice if that name was correct. It was her way of telling me she knows I'm married to Jim Nolan. She's been trying to get it out of him for a long time. They found it out somehow. I guess you know it too, Mrs. McCracken."

Maureen's throat felt dry, and she swallowed hard. Miss Huckstep knew she talked a lot in school. Now she'd find out Maureen had talked out of school, too.

Mama poured lemonade. "It was bound to come out, Alma, in a little place like Dotzero. But there's no law against a married woman teaching, and we're for you."

Mama could have put the blame right on Maureen, but she smoothed things over. Still, it might be the last day Miss Huckstep would be a teacher. School wouldn't be the same without her. Maureen watched Mit fill his plate. He wouldn't be at Dotzero School next year

135

either. She imagined a dark, rainy fall morning when she would have to get herself, Walter, and all of Uncle Millard's kids across the trestle without Mit.

If it had not been the last day of school, Maureen would have felt terrible. As it was, she didn't eat nearly as much as she should have, given an opportunity like the basket dinner.

15

Nobody expected Grandma to be ailing in summer after the flu and pneumonia season was over, but that's what Mama reported when she came home from Beaumont one day.

"I'll just have to go back prepared to stay a few days," Mama explained, as Maureen watched her pack a suitcase for herself and Walter. "Grandma is in a slump. Walter and I won't be gone long, just for a while to check up on your grandma. At her age, you can't tell. She might get weak, fall, and break a hip." Mama away was lonesome enough; now she was taking Walter. Since he'd almost died of appendicitis, Mama couldn't stand to have him out of her sight.

"Now, Mit, Dad will need your help. Maureen, do your best while we're gone."

"Even if Maureen does her best, we'll likely all starve," Mit predicted gloomily. "Time for a meal, Maureen's wandering around talking to herself or else

137

to the cellar door. I guess it doesn't matter, though, because she can't cook anyhow. When you're gone, Mama, Dad and I come in hungry from working hard and there's nothing on the table but the dirty dishes from the last meal we had to cook for ourselves."

"Oh, now, Mit, Maureen might surprise you," Mama said.

Maureen's eyes opened wide. Mama had hopes for her. Well, she'd surprise Mit and Dad with meals on time, and what's more she'd have a surprise for Mama, too, when she came home.

Much as Mama liked to work outside, she spent many hot summer days in the kitchen, canning fruits and vegetables. When other women told of how many quarts they had canned, Mama always had the most.

In her absence, Maureen decided to take over the canning job. When Mama returned, she would go down in the dim cellar and see jars of golden fruit filling a whole shelf. She'd be just dumbbellfounded at how hardworking and responsible Maureen had become.

Maureen knew just where to start. She'd seen early seedling peaches falling from a tree by the pigpen into the rank weeds below. She would can every last one of them.

After Mama and Walter had left to catch the train to Beaumont, Maureen was glad to have something to do so she wouldn't miss them so much. She tramped down the weeds and picked a half bushel of very small peaches. Some of them looked wormy and rotten on one side, but no matter. She could cut out the blemishes and they'd can up fine.

Tired and hot after that job, Maureen went into the cool sitting room and lay down on the floor. She was just dozing off when she began to itch. No wonder! Little black fleas jumped up from the rag carpet to gnaw on her. That was Walter's doing. If he wasn't watched every minute, he'd let Tisket into the sitting room to keep him company while he looked at pictures and tried to read Hurlbut's *Story of the Bible*.

Mama had left food to heat up for supper. That was about all Maureen could manage, what with scratching all her fleabites. At bedtime, she shook out her nightgown, but there were fleas in her bed all the same. She itched and scratched all night long.

When Maureen looked in the mirror in the morning, she knew she had more than fleas. The little blisters on her face and hands were from poison ivy. She had not noticed the three-leafed vine among the weeds when she'd picked up the peaches. Worse yet, she had spread the rash to all the fleabites she had scratched.

Well, that was the kind of thing you had to put up with when you kept house full-time, and the peaches still had to be canned. She'd finish the job after she put flea powder on the carpet.

It was a miserable morning. The sting of sweat made Maureen's irritated skin itch terribly. When she scratched, the blisters broke into red, swollen blotches.

The peaches were miserable too. By the time she peeled them and cut out the rot and the worms, there was hardly anything left. She was crying when Dad and Mit came in for noon dinner.

"I haven't got it ready yet," she wailed. "I didn't want these peaches to go to waste after I picked them up to can. Some I just have to throw away. I've got more to throw out than I have to kee-e-e-e-p," Maureen said, sobbing.

Dad examined her swollen hands and face. "You don't look in very good shape, Maureen. You've got an awful dose of poison ivy."

"I know. I got it yesterday, picking up these peaches. I didn't see it out there; the weeds were so thick and big. I wanted to have a lot of peaches canned up so Mama would be proud of all the work I'd done. But it was hot and then I got into a mess of fleas that must've just hatched out of the sitting room car-r-r-pet."

"That's what I call a peck of trouble." Dad looked at the basket of peaches and at the bucket of peelings, swarming with gnats. "But that's no peck of good peaches."

"I just have to go ahead and can some," Maureen insisted.

Dad looked at her eyelids. "Your eyes are about swollen shut with poison and cryin'. You might can us some little white worms if you can't see."

"I've got to show Mama." Maureen jerked with sobs.

"Now I'll show you what we're going to do with all this." Dad emptied the sloppy peelings on top of the little hard peaches. Through the narrowing slits of her swollen eyelids, Maureen watched him stride across the yard and barn lot and dump the whole mess into the pigpen.

What a wonderful thing to do! It made Maureen feel much better. She didn't even mind when Mit grumbled that now they had no peaches and no dinner either.

Dad mixed powdered sugar-of-lead and water in a little jar. He took a clean cloth from the rag bag and handed it to her. "Use this instead of your fingernails. Remember, it's poison, but I know I can trust you. Sop some on when you get to itching. I think the coolest place for you to be is out on the back porch. Stay out of the sitting room for a while."

It was cooler on the porch. The medicine made her more comfortable, but Maureen was disappointed that she hadn't reached her goal of the day. There would be no glowing shelf of canned peaches to show Mama. Mit was right. He and Dad would have to cook their own supper.

The salty tears that rolled down her cheeks hurt her irritated skin. She must stop crying. After all, Dad had trusted her with a jar of poison. That showed she was dependable. Maureen thought of her father's long strides across the yard and barn lot to heave those ornery peaches over the fence to the pigs. She would have smiled to herself if her face hadn't been so swollen.

16

The poison-ivy rash was drying up by the time Mama and Walter returned from Beaumont. Mama seemed to think that Maureen had gone out on purpose as soon as her back was turned and got herself plastered with itchy blisters. Maybe Mama didn't half listen to Maureen's explanation because she was still worried about Grandma, who had a bad case of being all out of heart. Mama considered that worse than tonsillitis or croup.

"I think it's because she'll be seventy her next birthday," Mama explained. "Three score and ten, that's a life-span according to Scripture. She kept quoting that text, saying it was the Gospel truth.

"She's far from well," Mama continued, "but I just had to get home, take care of our big gardens, do the canning, cook for the men. It's lucky school is out. That's where you come in, Maureen."

"What?"

"We've got a special job for you." Mama moved over to make room for Maureen beside her on the porch

143

bench. "Dr. Varney says Grandma shouldn't be alone just now. We want you to stay with her in Beaumont."

"Beaumont! I don't know any kids at all in Beaumont. Here I've got Walter. I wouldn't have anybody to play with in Beaumont."

Mama brushed Maureen's hair back from her eyes. "There won't be much time for play."

"But that's what I'm figuring on doing this summer. There are lots of things I want to show Walter. We're looking for something special, besides. He can't swim, so I'm going to teach him at least to dog-paddle this summer."

"We need you in Beaumont, Maureen."

"Can I go barefoot there?"

"No, best not in town, not an O'Neil."

"Can Walter go with me?"

"With my only girl away working, I'll need somebody here for company." Mama looked around the yard as if trying to see where Walter was. "He's had that operation. I need to keep tabs on him."

Maureen gazed at the cool woods above the sunny fields, then at the big barn backed by a fringe of orchard trees. "I want to stay at our farm, Mama, where I hear the bobwhite quails first thing in the morning and the whippoorwills last thing at night. Beaumont is all shoes and sidewalks."

"It's a lot to put on a girl your age, I know that. I like to be out in the cool parts of the summer days my-

144

self." Mama walked to the end of the porch for a better view of her gardens. "I wouldn't ask you to go if it wasn't important, Maureen. You have the spunk to be away from home to help. You got yourself in a pickle boarding the train, but you got yourself and Walter home. You talked to the dispatcher and stopped a big train for Walter. We're used to depending on you. You'd be staying with your own grandma."

Maureen fidgeted for a moment, then slid off the bench. "All right. I'll find Walter and tell him summer is not going to be the way we thought."

Walter was in the pasture, dragging a heavy hoe. "Dad gave me this pay job. I get a penny for every twenty-five thistles I cut down." Walter beamed. "I've already got one penny, and I'm starting on another."

"Walter, I hate to tell you this," Maureen said with a serious face, "but I have to leave home. I've got a sort of no-pay job in Beaumont staying with Grandma. It takes somebody dependable, so I ought to be glad I've got a chance at it. I won't have any time to play this summer vacation."

As Walter stared at her, Maureen left him and watched for her chance to slip into the kitchen and sit before the cellar door. "I won't be here again for I don't know when, Peloponnesus. For some reason I feel uneasy about staying with my own grandma. She's nice to me, brought me two barrettes for Christmas, and always sticks up for me because I'm an O'Neil and all. Still, it

145

will be just me and Grandma there in Beaumont. I won't have you or Walter to talk to. And then in no time, summer will be over and I won't have had any time to play or for Rose to come stay all night, or to learn if Miss Huckstep will be teacher, or to find an angel's egg. . . ." Maureen stopped, for someone was coming.

That was the last chance she had to talk to Peloponnesus. Mama kept her busy ironing all the dresses she was to take to Grandma's.

The day she left, Mama and Walter went along on Number 40, the early-morning train. They planned to stay in Beaumont all day and make sure Maureen was settled in at Grandma's. Mama cooked dinner, and the day was a nice one. But the scared, uneasy feeling almost overwhelmed Maureen when Mama and Walter walked down the street toward the Beaumont depot and she was left alone with Grandma.

Everything about Grandma's house was old. It smelled old—old dried-up varnish on old wood, old air in the rooms, old houseplants outgrowing their old pots and shutting out the light from the old windows.

Maureen soon discovered that Grandma liked to stay huddled up inside, but she escaped to the old front-porch swing whenever she could. As she pushed herself back and forth, she thought of Walter. Like as not, he would stop looking for an angel's egg. He would hoe down thistles and come to believe that the most wonderful thing in the world was a jar of copper pennies. Tisket would get ticks in her ears, and nobody would pull them out. Dad might slip into a black mood if she weren't there to prevent it. Maureen sorely felt she was more needed at home.

When she went inside and raised a window shade in the sitting room, Grandma pulled it down again so the sun wouldn't fade the carpet. Even in the afternoons, Grandma didn't wear any of her nice flowered dresses. Washing would fade them, too. Instead, she wore something she called a "wrapper." Maureen agreed that it was the color of brown wrapping paper.

Meals were awful. Grandma said nothing tasted good. There was no use cooking; she couldn't choke anything down. At first Maureen didn't feel like eating much either, but she soon grew hungry.

Eggs, biscuits, milk, and oatmeal—that's what a person was supposed to have for breakfast. Yet Grandma was sopping a store doughnut in coffee and then complaining about gas on her stomach. When Maureen was sent to the Kroger store, she bought oatmeal instead of the doughnuts Grandma had ordered. The next morning she followed the directions on the box and served Grandma a dish of hot oatmeal.

"Where are my doughnuts?"

"We're going to have oatmeal for a change. Now I'll tell you how I know about oatmeal, all the vitamins, minerals, and all that. I learned it listening to the eighth

147

grade. They have health. We don't have health in fifth. Now if you take minerals. . . ."

"Minerals!" Grandma snorted. "I'm not used to eating rocks and such."

She did take a couple of spoonfuls, however. Then she put her spoon down.

Maureen continued to talk. "Grandma, did you know Mit made the highest grade on the eighth-grade examination? Miss Huckstep said it was real good. Do you know Miss Huckstep?"

"One of Joe Huckstep's girls, I think. There was a raft of those Hucksteps. Her mother was a . . . never mind, I'll think of it directly. Now if you talk to me, speak up."

Maureen spoke louder. "The one I know, her name is Alma. She's right smack in the middle of her family. She told us that. There are four older than her and four younger. Now first there's Nathan. His nickname is Tate. He got that because the little kids couldn't say Nathan."

Grandma sighed, picked up her spoon, and took another bite of oatmeal. By the time Maureen had listed all the names, nicknames, and a few characteristics of each Huckstep, Grandma had finished her oatmeal.

Since they hadn't had eggs for breakfast, Maureen decided to fry some for noon dinner. Grandma watched her tap the egg on the edge of the stove to break it. Maureen had seen Mama do that many times. Then she stood back from the skillet, which held melted lard, and threw the egg in. Hot fat spattered on her hands while the yolk of the egg broke and ran over the white.

"Don't throw it in that way, as if you were killing a snake. Move the skillet over here, away from the hottest part of the stove."

Maureen grabbed the hot iron handle of the skillet. She shrieked, then jumped up and down with pain.

"No need to blister yourself." Grandma took hold of the hot handle with a crocheted pot holder shaped like a pair of drawers. "Cooking is not much fun if you're forever burning yourself. Always use a pot holder."

As soon as Grandma sat down to her egg and toast, Maureen began to tell her about the Sansoucies. "First chance I get, I'm going over to Cold Spring to see if they went to school the way they said they would. Rose wanted to go. Besides, I like to go there to play some good running games." Maureen gave the rules and ways to win all her favorite games.

While she talked, Grandma ate a pretty good dinner.

Supper didn't go as well, though. Maureen tried to make vegetable soup. While the vegetables cooked up to mush, the meat on the soupbone was too tough to eat.

"How do you get them to come out even, Grandma? It's like long division. I always know it's right if it comes out even."

"Oh, that's as easy as weeding after a rain. You start the soupbone an hour or so ahead. Then you boil the vegetables a few minutes in that good beef stock the meat cooked in. I'd have supposed your mother would have taught you that, same as I taught her. Hasn't she taught you to cook, Maureen?"

"Guess not." Maureen thought for a few seconds. "Mama likes to garden and work outside, but she's not much for teaching. Of course, maybe I was not very good at listening," she added. "One thing I've wondered. If you were cooking a rabbit, how would you get it done inside before it burned outside?"

"That's as easy as falling off a log. You brown it first over a hot fire. Then you pull it away from the heat some or turn down the burner if it's a coal-oil stove. You put a lid on it so its own steam will help cook it. And you turn it now and then and let it cook until it's tender."

"Same with fried chicken?"

"Yes, except with chicken, first you dip it in batter and then roll it in flour."

"Tomorrow I'll make us some," Maureen promised. She felt good about learning to cook. To do things, she had to take time to learn instead of being mad because she wasn't born knowing everything.

Maureen had to think of something to talk about as well as something to cook every mealtime. As long as she kept talking, Grandma kept eating. Things were tasting better every day to both of them.

150

17

Days were improving. Evenings were still lonely, especially when the train whistles blew. Maureen thought of the trains that rushed below her house at Dotzero, with their whistles moaning. It was still light when Walter's bedtime train went by. She thought of him catching lightning bugs by himself. He probably didn't miss her reading Hurlbut's *Story of the Bible* to him in summer. She wondered if Grandma had that book.

There was a bookcase in the sitting room, but it contained more knickknacks than books. The few on the shelves had small print and no pictures. Under a stack of quilt pattern booklets, Maureen found a photograph album. She marveled that the Grandma she knew, with her low, hoarse voice and spindly legs, had ever looked like the young woman in the yellowed photographs.

Grandma found her studying the pictures when she came in to pull down the sitting-room window shades. "I appear different on the outside," she said, looking

151

down at Maureen, "but I'm still the same person. It helps me if others remember that."

Maureen moved the books about on the shelf. "Have you got Hurlbut's *Story of the Bible?*"

"Got no such watered-down thing. I have the real Bible there on the table. It would be nice if you read me some Scripture, loud enough for me to hear. I quit going to church. Couldn't hear our new preacher." Grandma left the shades up and settled into a rocker.

No one except Walter and Miss Huckstep had ever asked Maureen to read before. Pleased, she opened the Bible and began.

"Not there," Grandma objected. "Too much slaying and slewing. I like Proverbs. Ecclesiastes, that's good too. Open the book right in the middle, and you'll find Psalms."

Maureen also liked the words of Psalms. Grandma was surprised at how well Maureen read. She set aside a time each day for Maureen to read Scripture.

At other times Grandma wanted neither reading nor conversation. She wanted to listen to news broadcasts on KSD. In a way, that was progress too. When Maureen had first arrived, Grandma wouldn't let her turn on the radio, although there was electricity in the house and no need to worry about running down the battery. She said she just did not want to hear "Fibber McGee and Molly" or "Guy Lombardo and His Royal Canadians" or anything.

Now Grandma turned up the volume and wanted everything as still as Dad did when he tuned in the livestock market report. Maureen heard about WPA and PWA and AAA and REA. It was like listening to the eighth grade at school; she learned a lot.

The letters that interested her most were PWA because she had seen them on a sign near Kroger's where men were building a curb. Grandma told her that towns all over the U.S.A. had PWA.

"How come we don't have it in Dotzero?" Maureen asked.

"Maybe because you never asked for it," Grandma allowed.

Maureen began to think. She was right there in Beaumont. Perhaps she could get PWA for Dotzero if she knew where to ask. The foreman on the curb job might help her.

Maureen needed a lot of nerve to talk to the man even if she did know about foremen from Dad's extra-gang job. He was the one that gave lots of orders and did little work. First she said howdy to him as she passed on her way to Kroger's. Then he began to chat with her and answer her many questions.

He explained that there was an awful lot of red tape involved in getting a PWA project. The application was enough to choke a horse. It had to show how many people were out of work, the need for the project, and the number of people to be served. The Beaumont

PWA office fielded it around for a while; then it went up to Jefferson City and even to Washington, D.C., itself.

Discouraged, Maureen was ready to give up the whole idea. She did use the information she'd learned to entertain Grandma at supper that evening, though.

That night Maureen dreamed of crossing the Dotzero railroad bridge. She was carrying one of Uncle Millard's kids piggyback. With all her strength she tried to lift her feet from the ties, but they wouldn't move. A train was coming. It whistled, and she could hear the bell clang as it came nearer and nearer. She awoke to hear the shrill whistle of a train engine at the Beaumont Main Street crossing.

Maureen told her dream to Grandma the next morning at breakfast. "I think it's a sign that we need a road bridge at Dotzero," Maureen said.

The Scripture reading from Ecclesiastes that day included the words, "A time to keep silent, and a time to speak." That was a second sign. Maureen knew she would have to speak for a bridge.

Carefully she got ready. She had a clean dress. Although her shoes were getting too tight, they looked fine with a little polish. She pinned wisps of her hair back with bobby pins while she tried out what she hoped was a smile rather than a grin before the dresser mirror.

On her way to the PWA office, she silently practiced her speech and kept on rehearsing it as she waited in the office for someone to notice her. After a long time, Maureen decided she could not sit forever in that waiting room, so she went into the inner office. The man in the white shirt at the big desk looked like the boss, so she marched up to him.

He looked up from a stack of papers. "What do you want, sister?"

"My name is not sister. It's Maureen McCracken of the Dotzero McCrackens. I want a bridge."

The man looked at her over the top of his glasses. He smiled and sat back in his chair as if he were ready to watch a good picture show. "Yeah, I remember Dotzero. Zero would be more like it. I used to fish down there on Lost Creek. Anybody still hanging around that place?"

"Yes, all us McCrackens and a big bunch of O'Neils moving in, too. All going to Dotzero School and have to cross Lost Creek to get there. If there was a bridge, folks from Post Oak could do their trading and catch the train in Dotzero. It would be a lot shorter for them than coming clear into Beaumont, wouldn't it? We need a bridge a lot more than you need a street curb in Beaumont. There's people out of work at Dotzero. They don't have to sleep under newspapers, but they can't pay the store bill or make an order to Sears or anything. They just sit on the store porch whittling on the benches and telling lies. Some of the kids haven't got decent clothes for school.

"So if they had work building the bridge. . . . It wouldn't have to be very wide, one-car wide would be enough. If ever two cars or a wagon got there at the same time, one could wait for the other, and it wouldn't need fancy banisters or anything. But it ought to be high, because Lost Creek comes up in a hurry.

"Everybody in Dotzero knows that. If we need a doctor now, we can't always get him across to tell us what sickness we have. Next time if it's anybody but Pat Ash at the depot, he might not stop the train the way he did for my brother Walter when he almost died with appendicitis. So instead of having everybody crying around at a funeral, we ought to have this bridge."

"Now hold your horses, Miss Maureen McCracken. All that may be so, but first an application form has to be filled out by a civic leader." The man in the white shirt laughed. "Of course, you wouldn't understand that term."

"Yes, I do. Eighth grade has civics, and I listen. It's somebody like Sterling Stackhouse, only he's no good. He wouldn't ask for a bridge unless all his kin and all his wife's kin got the jobs. I could fill it out. I've filled out orders to Sears."

The man shook his head. "I'm afraid that wouldn't work. But here's an application. You're all fired up.

You might get the community interested." He looked up at a map on the wall with a lot of pins stuck in it. "We don't have any projects down at that end of the county. More people and more needs elsewhere, I guess. Of course, we could make a stab at it and see if we get approval. There's a lot of red tape, you know."

Maureen nodded. Everybody was supposed to know about red tape, whatever that was.

Maureen was almost ready to turn off sizzling hot Main Street into a shaded walk when she recognized Miss Huckstep. Hot as it was, Maureen ran to meet her. "Miss Huckstep! I'm so glad to see somebody I know in Beaumont."

"I'm glad to see you, Maureen." Miss Huckstep moved into the shade of a store awning. "My, you look neat as a pin."

"You, too." Maureen admired Miss Huckstep's stylish ankle-length dress and her new hairdo, rolled in side sausages.

"I'm going to summer school. How is your grandma?"

"Perking up, Dr. Varney says. It's not as bad here in Beaumont as I thought it would be. I don't have to stay with Grandma every minute the way I did at first. This morning I went and got this." Maureen held out the application form. "Maybe you could fill it out. But first, tell me if you'll be our teacher again."

"I've not been hired, Maureen, but no one else has either, as far as I know."

157

SOUTHSIDE MEDIA CENTER
MORRISON, ILLINOIS

The time had come. Maureen felt she had to confess. "I'm the one that did it. I told Mrs. Stackhouse you were secretly married. She made me. She stood right there in the U.S. Post Office and made me tell that secret. Well, she didn't torture me or anything like that. At home they said a married woman wouldn't be hired. I'm the one told it. Do you hold that against me?"

Miss Huckstep dabbed her face with her handkerchief. "I did hope to teach, because I liked working with you kids. I'm still hopeful, so I'm going to summer school to keep my certificate up to date. Of course, you did a little unnecessary talking."

"I know. I read Scripture to Grandma this morning. It said 'a time to keep silent and a time to speak.' It was a time to keep silent." Maureen creased the folds of the application.

"And that's not so easy for you, Maureen, so no hard feelings. Now let's see what you have here." She took the form from Maureen and studied it.

"It's for a bridge over Lost Creek, right by the railroad trestle where we have to ford now. And there will be eleven more when Uncle Millard's family comes."

"Yes, the number of persons served is important. A couple of blanks ask for that information. Okay, I'll fill it out and turn it in. If I get stuck, I'll call on you, Maureen."

158

18

Grandma looked nice in her pink voile dress as she talked to Dr. Varney in the sitting room. It was bright and cheerful there with the window blinds raised. A spindly straight chair creaked under Dr. Varney's weight, and Maureen wished he had sat in the oak rocker.

He shook pills from a bottle into a little white envelope. "I'll leave you a few of these, but you may not need them."

"Oh, I know I'm a heap better. Getting my strength back, Doctor. Before Maureen came, I wasn't even tol'-able well. I had a bad spell. Trying to eat alone, day in and day out, I just about got out of the habit of eating." Grandma's eyes twinkled. "I think Maureen talked me into eating. Wasn't much else I could do while she rattled on. What a blatherskite! She got to be a real good cook, too."

"Now I think you can take care of yourself. I know that's what you want to do. Let's try it." Dr. Varney turned to Maureen. "Good young company can be better than medicine."

Maureen was pleased to be praised by Dr. Varney. Best of all, she knew she really had helped Grandma. They had helped each other.

A few days later Maureen went home to Dotzero on the train. There was nothing to it when she had a ticket.

Maureen was joyful as a fiddle tune just to be home. She pumped herself high and swung for a long time in the tire. It was good to go away once in a while, just for the happy feeling when she came home.

Maureen dramatized Dr. Varney's last visit for Mama and Walter. She took the parts of Grandma and the doctor, but left herself out. Naturally, she had said nothing while Grandma and Dr. Varney had bragged about her.

"We sent the right nurse," Mama said with a satisfied smile. "When Dad and Mit get home, you tell them how it went."

"You mean you *want* me to tell it again?" Maureen's cup was overflowing.

"Sure do. Everybody ought to know how you helped Grandma to take heart and be her old self again."

There were lots of changes at home. Mit's corn crop was waist high; spring chickens were frying size; potatoes, cucumbers, and green beans were ready to eat from Mama's garden. Walter seemed to have grown a little too. Dad had worked more days than he expected on the extra gang.

"We're about to see our way clear to buy the nails, roofing, and hardware for our addition," he said. "What do you think, Lillian? Shall we go to Millard's for the day soon? We can take a mess of garden truck to him and see if he's ready to come help butcher wood?"

"Good a time as any," Mama agreed. "Maureen's here to look after things."

"I've made a deal with Sterling Stackhouse," Dad explained. "You know, he's always looking for a bargain in wood to heat the store. We'll get some supplies from him in exchange for good, dry firewood; it's been stacked, drying for months. He likes to get it well ahead."

"I'm glad we don't have to charge anything this time," Mama said. "I don't like the way he slaps that store-bill pad down on the counter. We don't need much now with the hens laying, garden growing, but we can get flour, coal oil, and a little dry salt meat, too."

"Mit can haul the wood on the day we go," Dad said. "Then he can wait for the train and bring us, the supplies, and the grub home in the wagon all together."

A few mornings later Maureen rose at dawn with Mama. She got her feet and dress wet with dew as she helped gather a little of everything in the garden.

161

On the porch, they washed the root vegetables, picked over the lettuce, and carefully packed all the produce into two big splint baskets. "I feel as if we're going on a picnic today instead of to St. Louis," Mama said.

"Won't you have a lot to carry to the train?" Maureen asked.

Mama lifted a basket. "Not as heavy as those school books you carry home, and the walk's no farther than the one you kids have made to school many a time. Of course, by the end of this long day, we'll be ready for a ride home in the wagon along with our building supplies."

Mama, Dad, and Walter got an early start for their hike to the Dotzero depot. Mit had morning chores to finish before he left. As she washed the breakfast dishes, Maureen felt dependable, downright important.

She straightened up the kitchen and swept the back porch. It was still too early to start Mit's dinner. There was no one in the kitchen to overhear, so she turned to the cellar door to tell Peloponnesus about the PWA bridge.

Maureen gasped. The door was solid green. Peloponnesus was painted over. In the excitement of coming home, she had not noticed this change before.

Mit had started to load the wagon. Maureen could hear the clunk of stovewood as he tossed it from the pile near the yard into the wagon.

"Mit, oh, Mit," she called, as she ran outside. "What happened? Who painted the cellar door?"

Mit leaned against the wagon and grinned. "Somebody spoiled that loony game of yours while you were gone. A fellow, down and out, came up from the track and stayed here for a while. He was a house painter, so Mama bought some cheap paint on sale, and he painted different places around the house to pay for his keep. Mama likes all those colors."

"Well, I don't, and nobody asked me."

"I thought you'd be too useful now to waste time talking to yourself, Reen Peen." Mit sneered. "You could help me load this wood right now."

Maureen carried a stick of wood to the wagon. She was not as strong as Mit and could not throw it in the way he did. She hadn't told anyone at home about the bridge application. Now she couldn't tell Peloponnesus. She longed to tell someone.

"Mit, do you know we're going to get a bridge across Lost Creek? Not just a footbridge, a regular car bridge."

"Ha, ha, you make me laugh." But Mit wasn't laughing.

"It's so. We are."

"You're still going to get us a bridge? Ha, ha, what a laugh."

"Somebody does everything, Mit, and I'll tell you what I did when I stayed in Beaumont." Maureen tried

163

her best, but she couldn't convince Mit that the bridge would ever come to be.

It was discouraging. Mit was so stubborn. Everyone else praised her for saving Walter and helping Grandma out of a slump. Not Mit! Now that he had finished eighth grade and was through with school, he thought he was smarter than anyone else.

Maureen tried to toss the big chunks of wood with all her strength. "So when I stayed in Beaumont, I sure didn't know I'd get us a bridge. Then I met Miss Huckstep. You never know what's going to happen. That's what I tell Walter. I don't know exactly when we'll get it, do you? When do you think?"

"Never, so what's the use rattling on about it? Give your tongue and my ears a rest." Mit pointed to a black cloud in the south. "We're going to get a hard rain. Hurry, let's finish! I'll harness Fox and Jack in the barn and bring them here to hitch up. You can go with me if you stop blabbing."

It was going to storm for sure. Even Tisket could tell. She whined and stayed underfoot as Maureen tried to help Mit fasten the harness trace lines.

The storm had turned into a steady downpour by the time Mit reined the mules to a halt at Lost Creek ford. He and Maureen stared at the little creek in amazement. Swift, muddy water overflowed the banks.

Maureen held on to the wagon seat. "It didn't rain that much. What made the creek so high? What do you

think, Mit? Huh? What do you think? I tell you what
I think. I betcha it rained all night down around Post
Oak, and the water just got here. That's it. Don't you
think so, Mit? Our footbridge is gone—plank, chains,
stakes, and everything. You see that willow in the water?
That tree is supposed to be on the bank. I remember
that tree because Walter and I used to skip stones toward it."

Fox, the red mule, pawed and backed. "Whoa, whoa,
Fox." Mit pulled on the reins. "Maureen, will you
hush? Fox and Jack don't like this high water. Pipe
down, or we're going to have trouble. I've got two loads
of wood to haul. I want to get this one across now."

"We don't need to have trouble. Just let Fox and
Jack back up, back all the way up the hill home. I'll fix
us some dinner. We don't need to go plunging into that
deep water. And if I were you, Mit, I wouldn't—"

"You're not me." Mit looked up at the black sky.
"The longer we wait, the higher the water."

"I saw something like this in a picture show once.
Grandma and I went to it in Beaumont. They made
boats out of wagons. Of course, they didn't have a load
of firewood. Maybe—"

"This is no picture show. Now shut up." Mit clicked
his tongue and flipped the ends of the lines over the
backs of the mules. They moved into the water.

The wagon went down with a hard jolt. Water rose
halfway up the wheels. "It's all washed out!" Maureen

165

yelled. "It's way too deep. Turn them around! Turn them!"

"Can't," Mit muttered through clenched teeth.

"Then back them out, Mit. Back them out!"

"Shut up, can't you? Steady, Fox. Easy, Jack. Where's that shallow place?"

The wheels disappeared underwater. Just ahead of the mules, the current raced. Jack headed into it. Fox pulled back. Maureen was horrified to see the big rumps of both mules turn crosswise to the current. Jack thrashed in the harness, trying to swim. Maureen screamed. The wagon tipped, tipped, and went over. With chunks of heavy wood falling about her, Maureen went down into the swift, muddy water.

She tried hard to turn and get to the surface while she could still hold her breath. Which way was up? Something snagged her dress. With the strength and breath she had left, Maureen struggled free, pushed her head above water, and gasped for air.

She couldn't swim out of the swift current. All she could do was keep her head above water as she was swept downstream. Suddenly Maureen saw overhanging tree branches. She grasped a limb and with all her might pulled herself along it to the bank. She lay there, coughing up water.

When she had the breath to call, she screamed for Mit. His voice answered from someplace. Tree branches at the water's edge moved, and Mit came stumbling toward her. He was wild-eyed and appeared half drowned.

Far downstream, mules, harness, and wagon churned in the deep, strong current. "Whoa, whoa, steady Fox, Jack," Mit yelled. It was useless. He knew it. "They're drowning! Fox and Jack are drowning!"

Maureen saw Fox's red head come up and go down. Jack's black head didn't come up again. A few pieces of wood floated downstream. That was all.

"Fox and Jack are drowned, gone." Mit made a choking sound. "The wagon, everything gone. I'm not staying here, not after this. Maureen, you're good at talking. Tell Mama and Dad what happened to their team of young mules."

"Wait, don't leave me here by myself," Maureen pleaded.

Mit looked like a crazy person. He climbed on all fours up the railroad bank. Once he reached the track he started to run away from Dotzero two ties at a time.

The section crew filling in a track washout saw her first—Cleve McCracken's girl, wet and crying about a drowned team and runaway brother. They took her to the depot to stay with Pat Ash. He brought an old coat from the freight room and put it around her to try to stop her shaking.

Maureen sat and cried while she waited for the train to bring Mama, Dad, and Walter. Train sounds, people talking in low voices, Mrs. Stackhouse with soda water, clicking telegraph keys were all a jumble to her during the long afternoon.

Finally Pat Ash said, "It's in the block, Maureen. You better let me tell your folks."

She ran ahead of him to meet them as they got off the coach. They were shocked to see Maureen's torn, muddy dress and tearstained face. Dad grasped her shoulders. "What's wrong? Where's Mit?"

"Oh, it came! That awful day Mit talked about. It was today. Everything terrible happened!"

"What? What is it?" Mama cried.

"You folks better come sit down in the waiting room." Paul Ash led the way. "As you see, Maureen is all right, but there was a gully washer, the creek current shifted. . . ."

"Mit! Where's my boy?" Dad demanded.

"He's not drowned," Maureen said, sobbing.

"Oh, thanks be to God." Mama stumbled to a place beside Dad on the waiting-room bench.

"But the mules are. We don't have any more Fox and Jack." Maureen buried her face on Dad's shoulder.

"Near as I can tell, Mit must have miscalculated," Pat Ash explained. "The ford was washed out."

"Fox and Jack." Dad sounded stunned. "Good young mules, best in Dotzero. Just had them gentled down. I can't believe they couldn't swim out."

"Maureen says not, Cleve, says they pulled against

168

each other. Of course, scared as she was, maybe she's mistaken. They might have made it farther downstream."

"No, no, they didn't," Maureen insisted. "They're gone, and Mit's run away."

"He's probably home by now." Pat Ash tried to sound hopeful. "Or he will be by morning."

Mama stood up. "We'd better go see if he's there."

Dad didn't move. "Strange thing. I stepped off that train thinking everything was fine. The next second it's all changed. I guess I was born to be a poor man, never get ahead or be able to help Millard or anybody."

"Cleve, please don't talk that way," Mama begged. "We could have lost the children."

"I could get somebody to take you folks up to Lost Creek trestle," Pat Ash said.

Dad lifted Walter up onto his shoulders. "Much obliged, but we might as well start walking. We'll be doing a lot of it from now on."

19

Maureen awoke early the next morning and went at once to the boys' room. Mit's bed with the pillow plumped and the quilt unmussed was a dreadful sight to her. It meant that Mit had not come home during the night. He didn't come the next day either, nor the next.

Everyone around Dotzero was on the lookout for him. A farmer who lived three miles down Lost Creek found the carcasses of the mules. They were entangled in the harness, still hitched to a piece of the wagon. None of the families farming Lost Creek bottomland saw Mit, nor did anyone living near the railroad.

Maureen felt as if she had swallowed a stone. As each day passed, the stone felt heavier.

Mama stopped trying to drive away the black cloud of despair that overshadowed Dad. Instead of hoeing her garden, she sat idly on the porch staring down at the track. Sometimes she walked the floor, not talking to Maureen directly, but saying things like, "The good

Lord spared one of my boys and then took the other."

"Mama, Mit's not dead!" Maureen exclaimed. "He's off looking for work, maybe got something by now. He'll send us a postcard."

"It's terrible out on the road." Mama resumed her pacing.

Maureen thought of the homeless men she had seen from the train window, rows and rows of them wrapped in newspapers on a cold night. She tried to strengthen Mama's hope and her own, too. "But it's summertime. It'll be like camping out for him while he's looking for work. Maybe he'll go out West to the wheat harvest."

"Boys like him have it hard out on the road. I know." Mama started pacing again. "It's the young ones that come to the door to ask for a handout. The hard, older fellows wait on the track to take most of it. They figure most families can't refuse a youngster."

"I don't know why he ran away." Maureen sobbed.

"It was a lot to face. Mit knew we couldn't raise a crop, peddle apples or wood, or do anything without the team. We put too much on him, tried to put an old head on young shoulders. Now we're worn out with worry and got no help either."

"Well, when Uncle Millard comes," Maureen suggested, "then he. . . ."

"No more talk of that now. We wouldn't expect a bare-tailed possum to make a living in this Godforsaken place."

171

"Mama, our place is not Godforsaken! We live in the St. Francois Mountains."

"No more of that palaver, Maureen."

Their own hill, Godforsaken. Maureen hustled Walter outside so he wouldn't hear any more such talk. He was too little to get all out of heart. She urged him to keep searching for an angel's egg and even pointed out a white china doorknob in the trash pile for him to investigate.

Walter held up well enough except at night. Then Maureen could no longer drive the spook from the closet. Because Walter was afraid to sleep in the big room without Mit, Maureen slept in Mit's bed. Muddy water swirled through her dreams. Asleep and awake, she often saw the big haunches of the mules thrashing in the water. Mama thought dreams about muddy water meant bad luck. Apparently she was right.

Maureen wished Mama and Dad would come right out and blame her for the mules drowning and Mit's running away, just say that her jabbering had caused Mit to make a mistake. But they didn't. They just kept watching and looking anxiously whenever a man approached from the track to ask for something to eat.

As Mama didn't give her any jobs to do, Maureen often slipped away from Walter and wandered over the pasture and hayfield. She pretended she was talking to Mit. Yes, he was right. There would be no bridge. Without Uncle Millard's family, there would not be

172

enough people served. If Miss Huckstep had already sent in the form with the wrong count, it would land on the red-tape pile of requests containing lies.

Sometimes Maureen went as far as the Wiley place. She was poking around the yard there one day when Mrs. Wiley drove up. Maureen felt like ducking down behind the overgrown lilac bush, but instead she went to meet Mrs. Wiley and looked directly into her bright, sharp eyes. "I come over here every now and then to see if the house is torn down, but it's still here."

Mrs. Wiley pushed at the sagging fence. "Yes, but not for long. I'll give it a decent ending as it was the Wiley home place." She looked sharply at Maureen. "You're the one that helped your grandmother. She was telling me. Then I heard about your troubles. Any word from your brother?"

"Not yet, but he'll come up the hill home most any day now. He'll be back, but our mules won't ever be. Now we can't haul the lumber to build the rooms on our house for Uncle Millard and my aunt and nine cousins. They were going to move here from St. Louis because the box factory shut down in the city."

"Don't think the McCrackens and O'Neils alone have trouble." Mrs. Wiley shook her head. "You're not burdened with taxes on property as I am. No, indeed. I own most of the land in Dotzero School District, and I kept those taxes paid so that Dotzero School is in fine condition."

173

Maureen considered herself an absolute expert on Dotzero School. She could have told Mrs. Wiley about a broken windowlight and a loose floorboard under a certain desk.

"Whatever was required was forthcoming," Mrs. Wiley continued. "A drilled well, more windows, a woodshed, new fancy outhouses, maps, books—whatever those people in Jefferson City said that school had to have, my school taxes, all paid, provided."

Maureen wanted to tell Mrs. Wiley that she would like some new library books. But Mrs. Wiley was talking to her as if she were at least an eighth grader, maybe even a civic leader. Perhaps talking to somebody made Mrs. Wiley feel better. Maureen remembered the Scripture she'd read to Grandma. It was a time to keep silent. Maureen listened.

"Do you know what they say now?" Mrs. Wiley didn't wait for a guess. "They say we don't have enough pupils, claim Dotzero must be closed and the district go into Post Oak Consolidated. Of course, I know some have moved away, and for no good reason either, as it will be out of the frying pan into the fire. All the more attention for those, like yourself, remaining. But you should hear the arguments."

Mrs. Wiley flung up her hands in disbelief. "The children would have art and music and such." Mrs. Wiley snorted. "Wasting their time with daubs and scribbles. As for music, they get all the children tooting on horns. One or two can play a tune. The rest are just blowing their brains out. All that folderol costs money, don't forget. The school tax is much higher in Post Oak Consolidated District. It will bring me near ruin if the Wiley place and my other tracts go into that district and my tax bill goes even higher. Carting the children all over creation. I'm opposed to it." Mrs. Wiley's sharp eyes burned.

"Oh, I am too," Maureen agreed. "They have nine months of school at Post Oak Consolidated. They get scarcely any summer at all, not like Dotzero where we have eight months of school."

"High-handed I call it. Your folks must know of it, as the little tax you have to pay will also increase."

Maureen shrugged. "I don't know much about taxes. My folks haven't talked about taxes or about hardly anything much. Just thinking about Fox and Jack and the bridge we won't get and Uncle Millard can't come now, and worst of all, where Mit is."

"It's outrageous, just when he was big enough to help, start to pay for his raising, he ups and runs away. I thought it would put your grandmother back on the sick list. But, no, the surprising woman says she's coming to Dotzero for her birthday dinner, same as usual. I told her that if she had that much spirit, I'd drive her here myself and stay for dinner. I may look inside the house then, but not today."

Mrs. Wiley went to her car and just sat there behind

the wheel. She kept looking at the Wiley house. Maureen had started toward home when Mrs. Wiley called to her. "It's a crying shame about Millard and all those children. I know it's a great brood."

20

Maureen came home to find Mama still sitting on the porch. The *Capper's Weekly* that Maureen had brought earlier from the post office was on a chair beside her. She had not unfolded it to read one word of her continued story.

"Want me to do anything?" Maureen asked.

Mama shook her head.

"I saw Mrs. Wiley over at the old place. She says Grandma wants to come here for her birthday." Maureen put her arms around Mama. "Tell her No. I don't want to have a birthday dinner, same as usual."

"I know. I don't either." Mama sat up and straightened her shoulders. "You'll have to keep a stiff upper lip, Maureen. If Grandma wants to celebrate this birthday, we'll go ahead with it and put a good meal on the table. Anybody you want to ask?"

"Miss Huckstep, because maybe I'll never see her again."

"Never is a long time," Mama said. "I try not to

think of that word." Her voice softened. "I worry so about Mit. Then I reason that it's natural for young people to set out on their own. But he went too soon, went empty-handed, not even a change of clothes."

"I wish Mit would back up, get straightened out, come home, like a boxcar switched onto the right track," Maureen said.

That night Maureen dreamed of men wrapped in newspaper, lying on rafts that tossed on muddy water. The dream frightened her so that she fled crying into the next room to Mama's side of the bed.

"Sh-h-h, try not to wake Dad. He just got to sleep, and he has a day's work on the extra gang tomorrow. Every day counts. We've got to hold up for his sake. Think about what you are going to do tomorrow when daylight comes. I've found that helps."

Maureen went back to her bed and thought about going to the post office. She still had confidence in the U. S. mail and went everyday, hoping to hear from Mit.

The next morning Maureen and Walter waited at the postal window while Mrs. Stackhouse sorted the mail that Pat Ash had brought from the depot. Mrs. Stackhouse studied the address on a postcard. "You did get something here. It's not addressed to your folks, but to you, Miss Maureen McCracken. Postmarked yesterday, from . . . can't quite make that out." She turned the card over.

Maureen grabbed it from her fat fingers. She felt a

sickening wave of disappointment. The handwriting was not Mit's. It was an ordinary post-office card, no nice picture on the front. The card read: Dear Maureen, We are fine and hope you are the same. After you came to visit us, we went to school every day. We all passed. Come again right away. I know something <u>very important</u> to tell you. Your friend, Rose S.

On the porch, Maureen read the card twice to Walter. "You see how she's underlined very important?"

"Why didn't she write what it was?"

"Didn't have room maybe. Walter, we're going to the Sansoucies. This time we'll ask."

Mama said that if they wanted to make the long, hot walk on the back road to go ahead. One thing was sure, walking was the only way to get there.

Entwined with a blooming trumpet creeper and shaded by big maple trees the Sansoucies' house looked different in the summer. No one was playing in the bare, sunny part of the yard when Maureen and Walter arrived. At first, Maureen thought no one was home.

Then Rose came running from the shade. "I was looking for you, Maureen. I've got the kids pounding up rocks to make their own sandpile. You can help, Walter. The littlest ones are taking naps. C'mon, Maureen." Rose motioned and started walking away from the house. "We can't take the whole gang. I'll have to show you. It's by the tracks, not far from the water tank."

179

"What, Rose, what?" Maureen skipped to keep up.

"I think I saw Mit yesterday morning. It looked for all the world just like him, the glimpse I had before he took to the weeds and brush. I think he recognized us and didn't want us to see him."

As they headed for the track, Rose explained that the Sansoucie children had been picking blackberries along the railroad right-of-way. Berries were getting scarce, so they had gone farther from home than usual. "I didn't tell the other kids I'd seen somebody. They were scared because we weren't supposed to go that far and had seen a hobo fire. They wanted to get home."

Near the water tank, Rose stopped and pointed. "See that path off into the brush and briars? Hoboes stay down there, and when the engines stop to take on water, men come out and hop the freights."

"All right, Rose, wait for me here. I might do better by myself."

The weeds smelled rank as Maureen followed the path to a wide circle of trodden ground. Someone lay asleep near a pile of ashes and charred wood. It was Mit.

"Mit, oh, Mit, I've found you! Boy, am I glad!" Maureen shouted.

Mit roused and stared at her. His eyes were like burned holes in a blanket, and his black hair was dull with dust. He leaped to his feet.

Maureen grabbed him by the hand. "Mit, don't run

180

away again. Come home. It's just awful there now, as if somebody died, because you're gone."

"Fox and Jack died." He shook her hand loose. "Go ahead, blab to everybody that you saw me. But they won't find me. I'm getting out of here."

"Milton, won't you ever come home?"

"I'll be home when I can come leading a span of mules."

"Want me to blab that?"

Mit shrugged. "It's up to you."

"I won't, because Mama and Dad would feel worse. They don't care so much about the mules. Already they're getting used to no Fox, no Jack. They care because you ran away, acted as if they would hold losing the mules against you forever."

Maureen noticed that the toes of Mit's shoes were worn through and that his torn, dirty overalls hung on him. "You're skinny, Mit. Mama worries about how you're eating all the time. Where have you been?"

"I walked way up the other side of Beaumont, but there's no work there. So I came back here. Heard about this place at Cold Spring to hop a freight. I'm going to get out of here."

"Don't go, Mit. Dad's in such a blackness he might never come out of it. Mama's all out of heart. Walter pesters me all the time about when you're coming home. Tisket whines around. Grandma is holding up the best,

181

I guess." Maureen took a deep breath. "We're having a birthday dinner for her Sunday. It'll be real good. Different people are bringing things. She wants to bring something herself. Mama told her to bring deviled eggs. Only Grandma never says deviled anything. She calls them dressed eggs. Mrs. Wiley is going to drive Grandma to our house. She's bringing yeast rolls. Says they cost little and taste good, which they do.

"We'll fry up three or four spring chickens. They will be good with roasting ears just coming in and the first ripe tomatoes from Mama's garden. Miss Huckstep has a way of fixing new potatoes with creamed garden peas. She'll bring them and blackberry pie, maybe a meat loaf, too. Pat Ash is coming right after Number 3 so he can bring the ice cream packed down in ice that comes by express on the train.

"I'm going to make Grandma's favorite three-egg cake with chocolate frosting. I know how to do that now. So many hens are laying now that Mama will whip up a big angel-food cake and with the yolks left she'll make a sunshine cake. So there will be three kinds of cake. Which do you like best?" Maureen studied Mit closely.

Mit's eyes looked glassy. "Chocolate, only I won't be there, not with everybody saying, 'There's Mit McCracken, the one lost his Dad's good, young team.' "

"They'll be too busy eating to say any such thing. Everybody would be extra happy if you were home. Oh,

I forgot. We'll have homemade pickles, little sweet ones, and current jelly for the hot rolls, and Molly's butter, and crocks of sweet milk, and a couple pitchers of lemonade. It's this coming Sunday."

"What day is today?" Mit croaked.

"Thursday, so you might as well come now. Then we could all go home together."

Mit stirred the cold ashes with a stick. "No, guess I'll not come. Just go ahead and have your big feed."

Maureen hated to leave Mit there alone, but she knew she needed help to persuade him to come home. She pushed aside the weeds beside the path and returned to the track where Rose patiently waited.

"You saw him all right, but it's a wonder you knew him. He looks so different, Rose, and he says he's moving on. Walter and I can't stay to make sand. I'll have to get home and tell Dad where we saw Mit. I tried, but I don't know if I did any good or not."

A train whistled for the Cold Spring crossing. Rose and Maureen stood close to the right-of-way fence and watched the freight slowly glide into the water-tank siding. "I think Mit is still trying to get up nerve enough to hop a train," Maureen said, "so maybe there's time yet."

21

Walter's bedtime train went by, but Mama let him stay up and wait for Dad. He had been gone for hours to search for Mit. Mama was lighting the kitchen lamp when they heard footsteps on the porch. Lamplight shone on Dad's face; they did not need to peer into the darkness beyond the door to know he was alone.

"Any trace, Cleve?" Mama asked.

"Just a fellow at the hangout. He said a youngster like Mit had shagged out of there."

"I should have made him wait," Maureen said.

"You did your best, Maureen." Dad stroked her hair and brushed some wisps out of her eyes. "You couldn't hog-tie him. I can search every hobo jungle on the railroad, but I can't drag him home by the scruff of the neck. He's got to come round to it himself."

It was the most Dad had said for a long time.

Mama looked ready to cry. "I was so in hopes he would be here Sunday for Grandma's birthday. Wouldn't that have been a surprise?"

"I told him about it. I told him," Maureen repeated.

"We'll go through with it same as usual, even if we don't feel like it." Mama sighed.

On Sunday Mama wanted the plank table set out in the shade. Grandma and Mrs. Wiley were the first to come. Grandma didn't act like company. As spry and handy as a pocket in a shirt, she put an apron over her flowered dress and helped with dinner.

Maureen's last task was to make sure the number of seats and plates matched the number of people. She was careful to check that there was an extra setting, in case it was needed. Just before everyone sat down, she went to the edge of the yard for one more look toward the track. Mit was not coming. It was all Maureen could do to keep a stiff upper lip.

Grandma gave thanks for the food. She gave thanks for the years she'd had and for the ones she was expecting. Then she asked God to look after all of her family—in the big city and abroad in the world, wherever they were. It was enough to make a person bawl.

Jim Nolan sat beside Miss Huckstep, who was taking second helpings when she announced, "I want to tell you that I'll be teacher at Dotzero next term. That's what Sterling Stackhouse tells me. He and the like-minded board members have decided to let an old married woman teach."

Mama passed the chicken. "Why the change of heart?"

"His niece got rehired for one thing. For another, he's finally sure our school meets all the state requirements. Mostly, I think he's grateful to me for applying for the bridge. I'm happy to tell you that the project has just been approved. Mr. Stackhouse says it will bring him more paying trade."

Dad looked at Maureen with astonishment. "That bridge Maureen told us about? I never thought it would go through."

Mama laughed. "Maureen had that dream where she falls off the trestle once too often, so she spoke up and did something about it."

Miss Huckstep beamed at Maureen. "She learned to use her gift of gab."

Everyone was laughing and talking at once, glancing with admiration at Maureen. But she was silent; she knew the good news wasn't true. There were not enough children for a school at Dotzero. There were not enough people for a bridge.

Maureen looked up when she heard Mrs. Wiley clear her throat. She too wished to make an announcement. "I've been thinking of the Millard O'Neil family. They are welcome to move into the Wiley place, rent free, if they want."

Dad dropped his fork. "Do you mean that, Mrs. Wiley? That's uncommon generous."

"They would be better off here with the rest of you."

She waved her hand over the table. "Be able to raise food as you do. Of course, I'd expect some repair on my house in place of rent, nail up a loose board now and then."

"That's wonderful!" Mama smiled and cut more cake. "Now I'll have some good news to write to them."

Grandma took another piece of chocolate cake. She looked over and patted her friend's hand. "Mrs. Wiley, I never thought of you as an instrument of Providence, but in this case I believe you are."

There was enough food for everyone to take some home and still leave plenty. Mama wanted to let the dishes wait for a while so she could get out her tablet and write to Uncle Millard. Maureen had figured something out and was bursting to talk, but she decided to stay outside with Walter until Mama finished her letter. She was giving Walter his turn in the swing when she saw someone coming up from the track. She knew that walk; it was Mit.

Walter slid out of the tire and ran to grab Mit around the legs. Tisket had a fit of joy. Maureen was speechless.

"Anything left to eat? What's the matter, Maureen? Didn't you expect me?"

Maureen ran toward the house, shouting, "Mama, Dad, it's Mit! He's home! He came round to it!"

Mama began laughing and crying. She just about ruined a page of her letter with tearstains.

The dark expression left Dad's face as he looked at Mit. "You've taken a heavy load of worry off us, just the sight of you."

"I aimed to stay away until I could come back leading a span of mules." Mit grabbed Walter and tickled him. "Then I thought Walter would be grown up by then. I got so lonesome I even missed Maureen's blatherin'. And I got so hungry I could have eaten her cooking."

"You'll be surprised." Mama looked proudly at Maureen. "Things don't always stay the same."

"Then when Maureen and Rose bird-dogged around and found me, Maureen talked me into coming home," Mit continued.

"Maureen did that?" A big smile spread over Dad's face.

"It didn't work right away, but the closer Sunday came the hungrier I got."

Mama jumped up. "What am I thinking of?" She quickly started filling a plate for Mit. As she watched him shovel in food, she said, "You must have learned a lot out on the road."

"Learned there was a lot I didn't know. I can't do the work of a mule team, but I can earn my keep."

Mama filled his plate again. "There's a job for all of

us now. We've got to get the Wiley place fit to live in. Mrs. Wiley says Millard's family can live there rent free."

"Things *don't* stay the same! Mrs. Wiley! Are you sure?" Mit gulped down a glass of milk.

"Well, I can tell you why. . . ." Maureen began. Then she stopped. She could have gone on and explained what she had figured out. It was like a long-division problem that came out even. Mrs. Wiley had given the house to Uncle Millard's family so there would be enough kids in the district to keep Dotzero School open and her taxes down. But if Maureen told that, everybody would go back to thinking Mrs. Wiley was as close as the bark on a tree, mean, and kept kids from tooting horns at Post Oak Consolidated. Mrs. Wiley had saved the bridge and saved Maureen from a month of extra school. Besides, she was an instrument of Providence, according to Grandma. Maureen was grateful to her. It seemed one of those times it was best to keep silent.

"Tell what?" Walter asked.

"Why I want you to come finish your turn in the swing," Maureen said, pulling him away from the others.

"A lot of good things happened today, Maureen, but we won't ever find an angel's egg like Peloponnesus said. He's gone, painted out."

189

"Oh, no, he's not, Walter. Peloponnesus is under the paint. Things are not gone just because you can't see them."

Walter smiled until his eyes closed. "Okay, then I want to show you something."

Near the fence, Walter stooped beside a patch of bare earth. A smooth, rounded white form bulged from the ground. "Maybe this is it." He worked his fingers around the white bulge.

"Careful, careful, Walter."

His short fingers slipped under an edge. He pulled out a jagged shape resembling a broken bowl. They both stared at it.

"It has already hatched," Walter whispered.

Maureen sighed with satisfaction. "Just think, it hatched out here at the McCracken place on Lost Creek in the St. Francois Mountains during the Depression."

They gazed up at the last rosy clouds in the evening sky. One was shaped just like an angel Maureen had seen in the colored glass window of the Beaumont Methodist Church.

About the Author

Marian Potter was born in Blackwell, Missouri, fifty miles south of St. Louis. After attending public school in DeSoto, Missouri, she went to the University of Missouri at Columbia, where she graduated with a degree in journalism. Her professional writing experience is very diverse, including staff and free-lance work in broadcasting, advertising, industry, and journalism. In addition, Ms. Potter is the author of several books for children, among them the recent novel *The Shared Room*.

A mother of three, and grandmother of two, Marian Potter now lives with her husband in Warren, Pennsylvania.